"Do not tell me you
are shocked, Carey!"

The thickness of Dimitri's voice
suggested that his passion had not
abated. "I can't believe this is the first
time you've been kissed."

Carey felt so shaken she couldn't reply.
She had never in her life behaved as
she'd just done with Dimitri. "I'm—I'm
not in the habit of kissing every man I
meet like this," she finally managed to
stammer.

"Was it not what you expected?" The
dark eyes held captive her own.

"Not from you—my employer!"

"I've never yet apologized for kissing a
pretty woman," he told her in a flat
voice, "and I'm not going to make you
the exception." To prove his point he
bent and once again pressed his mouth
to hers....

Dark Enigma

by

REBECCA STRATTON

Harlequin Books

TORONTO • LONDON • LOS ANGELES • AMSTERDAM
SYDNEY • HAMBURG • PARIS • STOCKHOLM • ATHENS • TOKYO

Original hardcover edition published in 1981
by Mills & Boon Limited

ISBN 0-373-02466-5

Harlequin edition published March 1982

CHAPTER ONE

CAREY had never been more nervous in her life before, and yet whenever Niki looked at her with his enquiring dark eyes she somehow managed to smile reassuringly. It wasn't easy, but she felt she had to keep up an air of confidence, because Niki was only six years old and his whole world had been turned upside down.

She hadn't yet dared anticipate how she was going to break the news to him that when they reached the end of their journey she was to hand him over to strangers and then vanish from his life for good. For four of his six years she had been the most important person in his life, for his mother hadn't the time to give him the care and attention that bringing up a small boy required. The parting was going to be hard, and the nearer the moment got, the more Carey dreaded it.

Aliki Karamalis, Niki's mother, had been such a vivid and volatile character that it was difficult to believe she had simply ceased to exist. She had seemed too vital to have died so young and Carey still had difficulty accepting it. Aliki had been born in Greece of a well-to-do family and had left home with the hope of making a career for herself in England as an actress, but within a few months of her arrival her stage ambitions had been forgotten when she fell in love with an Englishman almost twice her age.

He was a married man and there was no question of a divorce, so Aliki had subdued her not inconsiderable pride and taken the only alternative, even though it had meant cutting herself off from her family. That had been hard, but she had stuck to her decision and never attempted to contact them again, and when Niki, her son, had been born less than a year after the affair began, her family

were never informed. By the time he was two years old
Aliki had decided that the combined roles of mistress and
mother did not work for her, and she had counted herself
lucky to get someone like Carey Gordon to look after him.

Carey was small and fair and very pretty, a complete
contrast to Aliki's dark sultriness, and yet the two had
eventually become close friends, despite their very different
life-styles. Carey had been at her bedside when Aliki died
of pneumonia only weeks before her twenty-ninth birth-
day; no one else had come, and it was to Carey that she
entrusted her son.

'Take him to my family in Greece, please, Carey,' she
had begged. 'I have written a letter for Dimitri which you
can take with you, and I know he will care for him even
though I have brought disgrace on them. He may have
sons of his own now, I do not know, but he will take Niki
for my sake; I know my Dimitri.'

It was an appeal that was impossible to resist, even
though the idea of travelling all that way turned Carey's
knees to water; she had never been abroad before, and
Greece seemed an awfully long way to go. She had put a
lot of thought into the letter she sent Dimitri Karamalis,
for one thing because it wasn't easy writing to a complete
stranger and explaining the situation as well as announc-
ing their imminent arrival.

It had been necessary to act quickly, for now that Aliki
was gone, so was her income, and Niki's school fees alone
were more than her month's salary had been. If Aliki's
family were willing to support the boy, they were hardly
likely to do the same for her and she would need to look
for another post as soon as possible, although it was
something she didn't want to think about too much at
present.

She had explained as best she could that they were
going to Greece to see his mother's family, but she didn't
think Niki fully appreciated what was to happen, and she
had not yet summoned the nerve to tell him the plain

truth. So far he had enjoyed all the hustle and bustle of travelling, and if he was a bit bewildered by it all he didn't complain but chattered happily to her as he pointed out the different things that took his eye.

They were coming in to land at Athens airport, and while Niki shrilled happily about the ground coming up to meet them, Carey again felt the now familiar flutter of panic at the prospect ahead. Everything looked so incredibly bright and beautiful from above, and she was dazzled by the impression of white buildings and green hillsides so that for a moment her heart beat with a different kind of excitement.

The sun was hot and flamboyant, quite unlike the mellow English sun, and she leaned down to look past Niki, out of the window. 'It won't be long now,' she told him, and briefly he turned from the window and frowned curiously.

'We here?' he asked as the plane rolled to a stop and the engines cut out.

'We're here,' Carey confirmed. Her legs were shaking and she felt an overwhelming sense of anticipation and apprehension as she got to her feet and reached over to help Niki from his seat. 'Hold tight to me,' she told him as they followed in the wake of the other passengers, and he needed no second bidding for they were surrounded by strange faces.

'Where is this?' he asked as they stood shortly afterwards in the reception area.

'Athens, darling, where Mummy was born.'

Perhaps it hadn't been very wise to mention his mother at that point, but she was feeling anxious about their being met. There had been no time to wait for a reply from Dimitri Karamalis, so she could only assume that someone would be coming to meet them, and she looked around anxiously. All Niki's possessions were in the two suitcases alongside her, and her own things, as many as she would need for a few days stay while things were sorted out, were in another, smaller case at her feet, and she was beginning to have the awful suspicion that no one was coming.

It was so warm that she wished she had worn something more light and summery, but the English summer had been nowhere near as warm, and the blue linen dress with half-sleeves had seemed ideal. Niki was beginning to show signs of restlessness in the anti-climax of arrival, and Carey took note of his out-thrust bottom lip anxiously. He wasn't normally badly behaved, but he must be tired and probably hungry too.

'Why are we waiting here, Carey?' he wanted to know, and she smiled encouragingly.

He was a small, chubby boy and rather too pretty for a boy, but his mother had assured her that he would grow up to be handsome like all the Karamalis, and she was probably right. 'For your uncle to come and fetch us,' she told him. 'Or maybe he'll send someone else, but someone will be coming for us very soon now.'

'Uncle Dimitri?'

Carey noted thankfully that he coped very well with the unfamiliar name, and she nodded. 'That's right, darling—Uncle Dimitri.'

'Will you accept Uncle Mitso instead?' Carey swung round quickly to see who had spoken, and found herself facing a tall, dark and very good-looking young man, only a few years older than herself, and therefore not Dimitri. 'Miss Gordon?' He beamed her a sparkling-white smile, and Carey nodded a little dazedly. 'I am Mitso Karamalis—welcome to Greece!'

Aliki's youngest brother; she would have known him for a Karamalis because he was very like Aliki, but his manner was slightly disconcerting in the present situation. He had thick black curling hair and dark eyes that looked at her with a glint of impudence as well as appreciation, and he took her hand when she offered it, but raised it to his lips instead of simply shaking it.

'And this is—Niki, yes?'

Niki shook hands solemnly, but he frowned instead of smiling, obviously puzzled by the different name, and his big round eyes watched the man warily. 'Not Uncle Dimitri?' he asked, and Mitso Karamalis laughed.

'No, little one, I am Mitso.' He was a bold and uninhibited character and in her mind Carey tried to imagine him condemning his sister for her unconventional love affair, and couldn't. Mitso Karamalis didn't look the kind of man to disapprove of the situation, but rather as if he might indulge in it himself. 'Dimitri leaves such mundane matters as meeting planes to others,' he explained in very strongly accented English, 'and since I am the least important member of the household then I am here to meet you.' His expressive dark eyes took stock of her with a bold intensity and he smiled broadly. 'In this instance I am very pleased to have been—delegated,' he told her in a voice that was surely meant to send little shivers of sensation along her spine. 'I have a car outside, Miss Gordon, if you will please come with me.'

In a matter of minutes the suitcases were stowed in the boot of a huge black Mercedes and Niki was installed in the back seat, while Carey sat beside Mitso Karamalis. 'Where we going now?' Niki wanted to know, and their guide turned his head briefly and gave him a broad wink.

'To find your Uncle Dimitri,' he told him, then immediately gave his attention to Carey once more. 'I am sure you will like Greece, Miss Gordon, it is very beautiful.'

'So I've heard.'

In fact she wasn't very impressed with their present venue as they drove through some rather run-down suburbs, but Mitso Karamalis was shaking his head. 'Do not judge by what you see here,' he told her. 'When we have travelled a little distance you will see what I mean. You are going to enjoy living in my country, Miss Gordon.'

It wasn't the time to tell him that she wasn't staying with Niki, but she wanted no misunderstandings and Niki

was pretty well occupied at the moment with watching
the traffic and the mass of people in the hot, sunny streets.
Hoping that Mitso Karamalis would do the same, she
kept her voice as low as she could and still be heard. 'I'm
sure I would, Mr Karamalis, but——' She gave a brief
checking glance over her shoulder. '*I'm* not staying in
Greece; at least for no more than a day or two until Niki is
settled in. Oh, I don't intend imposing myself on your
family, naturally, I'll find a room somewhere.'

Mitso Karamalis gave her a long look from the corner
of his eyes, then shrugged. 'You will find that it is all
arranged, Miss Gordon. You are to stay at the villa,
Dimitri has arranged it so.'

So Dimitri had arranged it so. From the sound of him
Dimitri Karamalis was a man who called the tune and
expected others to dance to it, but Carey preferred to
make her own plans. Staying under the same roof with
Niki would only prolong the agony of the eventual parting,
and it was going to be hard enough as it was. If she was
too close at hand he was going to cling to her among all
those strange faces, and she had to harden her heart for
both their sakes.

'I don't think Mr Karamalis quite understands the position,' she said, and passed an anxious tongue over her lips
before going on. 'It's very kind of him to suggest I stay for
a while, but I have to go back, and the longer I'm here
the worse it will be.'

For a moment a glimpse of compassion showed in the
bold dark eyes, and a hand pressed over hers. 'That is
understood,' he assured her. 'That is why Dimitri wishes
you to remain.'

'Also I have to look for a new post very soon,' Carey
insisted. 'I can't afford to stay too long, to be perfectly
honest, Mr Karamalis.'

His broad shoulders shrugged carelessly and the full
lower lip pursed as if in doubt. 'Best to tell it to Dimitri,'
he suggested.

Despite their efforts at keeping their voices down the gist of what they were saying eventually dawned on Niki in the back seat, and he stood just behind Carey with one hand on her shoulder, his dark eyes big and anxious as he sought reassurance. 'You're coming too to Uncle Dimitri's, Carey? You must come too.'

She glanced at the man beside her but saw only a certain satisfaction on his face, and wondered if he had any idea of the spot she was in. 'It seems you have little choice, eh?' he suggested.

Carey reached for the hand that rested on her shoulder and squeezed the small fingers reassuringly. 'Of course I'm coming too, Niki,' she said, and felt somehow as if she had burned her bridges with those few words.

It was getting on towards evening when they drove the last few kilometres, and Carey had to agree that Greece was indeed beautiful. It was one of the most fertile areas in the country, Mitso assured her, and when she looked at the rolling hills covered in olive trees and grapevines and orchards it wasn't hard to believe.

'It's beautiful,' Carey said softly, and didn't realise she had spoken aloud until Mitso Karamalis half turned his head and smiled.

'Did I not say so?' he asked.

'I'm a complete novice where foreign travel is concerned,' she confessed. 'I've never been anywhere overseas before.'

'Then you must learn all about Greece while you are here,' Mitso told her. 'I shall give myself the pleasure of showing you, Miss Gordon.'

Which sounded all very nice, Carey thought ruefully, but she wasn't there to take a holiday whatever this handsome Greek believed. If she didn't find herself another job very soon she would be in dire straits, and apart from refunding her fare she did not imagine Dimitri Karamalis would consider himself any deeper in her debt.

Choosing to ignore the suggestion rather than argue about it, she took a different line. 'Aliki told me quite a lot about it at various times,' she said, and added, 'I was very fond of Aliki.'

There was a brooding sadness in the dark eyes for a moment, and he shook his head slowly. 'We loved her,' he said, and Carey could not help asking herself what kind of love it was that turned its back on an errant sister and daughter. Turning the car into a tree-shaded, narrow private road he brightened again and pointed ahead. 'Did Aliki also tell you of our home?' he asked. 'We are arrived, Miss Gordon.'

Carey's heart gave a sudden lurch of panic as she looked along the narrow winding road ahead, and she gripped her handbag a little more tightly as the prospect she had dreaded so much loomed ever nearer. But it was beautiful, she could not ignore that even though she shook with nervousness and her stomach felt churningly queasy.

The sky had turned to a glowing gold and gilded the hills behind the villa with a Midas touch that also touched the glimpses of white walls that showed between the trees. All along the road on both sides grew thick borders of orange and lemon trees and in front of them a mass of flowering shrubs, most of which she didn't attempt to put a name to. Jasmine, hibiscus and oleander, she recognised, and in the warmth of the evening sun the perfume from them was as heady as wine.

Then they were facing the house itself suddenly. Passing through a row of guardian cypresses the glimpses she had caught earlier became a reality, and she caught her breath. It was huge and dazzlingly white with a row of tall, fluted columns in front so that it put her in mind of a Greek temple, and the gardens surrounding it grew with the colour and profusion of a garden of Eden.

All the same trees and shrubs that had lined the road and a lot more besides, as well as a mass of bedding flowers, rioted in every direction. No one, Carey consoled herself as they drove up to the house, could be anything but kind and compassionate living in surroundings like these.

When Mitso braked the car to a halt she was still staring as if she could not believe her eyes, and she automatically accepted his hand to help her out of the car. Only when she felt Niki's hand in hers did she bring herself quickly back to earth and smile at him. 'We're there?' he asked, and she nodded.

'Yes, we're there, darling. Isn't this a lovely house?'

Niki gave a curious little shrug that was entirely Greek. He wasn't old enough yet to be influenced by trees and flowers and beautiful architecture, and he looked up sharply when Mitso Karamalis slipped a hand under Carey's arm with easy familiarity. Together they all three climbed the white marble steps that led to a door standing wide open as if in welcome, and Carey's heart at least prayed that there would be a welcome for them.

The outside of the house had impressed her, but the inside dazzled her, for the reception hall they walked into was even more reminiscent of a Greek temple. There were slim Doric columns supporting a high ceiling, and a floor tiled in a pattern of blue and white, and all around, in shallow niches in the walls stood white marble figures in classic Greek dress. A wide staircase rose from the centre of the hall and several doors leading off suggested that this was the heart and hub of the whole villa.

Carey had to admit to being overawed as she followed Mitso Karamalis across the blue and white tiled floor, and she could feel Niki's hand in hers gripping tightly as he trotted along beside her. 'Carey.' He tugged at her hand to attract her attention, and when she looked at him, smiling automatically, she noticed how tired and heavy-eyed he looked. 'Carey, I don't like it here much, can't we go home?'

His uncle stopped and looked down at him, and Carey noticed the speculation that showed in those bold, impudent eyes for a moment. Half-smiling, he shook his head at him. 'You *are* home, *àgóri*,' he told him, and laughed suddenly. 'You will grow accustomed to it, you have no choice, eh?'

It was a harsh judgment, and if Carey had been better acquainted with the man who made it, she would have told him so, as it was she gave her attention to comforting Niki. His lip trembled and he turned and buried his face in the skirt of her dress. 'I don't like it here,' he insisted in a small muffled voice. 'I want to go home.'

'Oh, Niki!' She hugged him close, for her own eyes were misty and if he noticed it would make matters even worse. 'Be a good boy and don't cry, darling. We—we can't go back to London but this is a very lovely house and it—it'll soon seem like home, you'll see.'

But at the moment he couldn't see, and Carey was feeling so travel-weary herself that she again felt that surge of panic that had showed itself so often on the journey there. These exotic surroundings, and the bold, speculative look in Mitso Karamalis's eyes were so alien to her that her instinct was to gather up Niki and go straight back home to England. Standing in the middle of that great hall she felt lost and rather helpless, and she turned her head sharply when one of the doors opened and another man came out.

He was tall and very dark and rugged rather than handsome as Mitso was, and as he came towards them Carey had no doubt she was about to meet Dimitri Karamalis. His air of arrogance suggested he was quite capable of organising other people's lives, as Mitso suggested, and of deciding that she should stay at the villa, whether or not she wanted to.

There was a strength in his features that was lacking in Mitso's good looks, and his body had the lean hardness of an athlete, with broad shoulders, narrow hips and long muscular legs that brought him across the hall in lengthy impatient strides.

'Miss Gordon?' He didn't wait for his brother to introduce her, but thrust out a large hand, and there was no smile of welcome either, only a frankly curious survey that took her measure while his long fingers clasped hers tightly. His eyes were disconcertingly black, she noted, not merely dark as Mitso's were. 'I am Dimitri Karamalis.' He looked down at Niki with his face still hidden in her skirt and Carey noticed no appreciable softening of the lean features. 'This is my nephew?'

'Yes, Mr Karamalis.' She put a hand under Niki's chin and managed to persuade him to lift his face, but he wouldn't let go of her. 'This is Niki—Nikolas Dimitri. Aliki always spoke of you as her favourite brother and she named Niki for you.'

He acknowledged the tribute with a barely perceptible nod, and Carey was uneasily aware that Mitso was smiling to himself, as if the situation amused him. 'The boy is obviously tired after the journey,' Dimitri Karamalis decided. 'He should go straight up to his room; introductions can be made later when he is more rested. Katina will look after him for the moment; give him something to eat and some milk, and then put him to bed, hmm?' He spoke to Niki in Greek and Carey realised that this was another moment she had been dreading, for Niki again hid his face.

Placing a protective hand on his head she drew him close, making her explanation in a quick and slightly breathless voice. 'I'm afraid Niki speaks English more readily than Greek, Mr Karamalis; you see he's spent most of the past four years with me, and Aliki—his mother, mostly spoke English because Niki's father didn't know Greek.'

She wasn't at all sure of the wisdom of speaking about Aliki when Niki was so close to tears, but explanations were necessary and in fact Niki had been more attached to her for the past years than he had to his mother. 'So,' Dimitri Karamalis said with obvious dislike, 'we have a Greek boy who speaks only English.'

It was a harsh judgment in Carey's opinion, and she hastened to Niki's defence automatically. 'Oh, that isn't quite true,' she said. 'He has a little Greek and I'm sure he'll soon pick it up.'

'It is to be hoped so, *thespinís*!' He turned and said something to his brother and, with a slight shrug of apology, Mitso left them. 'I have asked that Katina our—housekeeper?—come and take the boy to his room, and for one of the maids to show you to your room, *thespinís*,' Dimitri went on. 'You will no doubt wish to refresh yourself before the evening meal, after which we shall wish to hear what you have to say about this situation.' She had no time to say anything before they were joined by a short, stout middle-aged woman, and a young girl who lingered somewhere in the background. 'Katina will attend to you,' he told Niki, 'go with her.'

'No!' Niki, instead of doing as he said, clung to Carey more tightly than ever, and his huge dark eyes appealed to her not to send him away.

'But you're very tired, darling,' Carey told him gently, doing her best to resist the appeal. 'You can have a glass of milk and something to eat and then go to bed.' She held him firmly away from her because this was going to be the first break and she had to be firm about it. 'You'll be all right, darling, don't worry.'

'But you *always* come with me,' Niki insisted with a trembling lip. 'Please, Carey!'

He still kept a hold on her dress and he darted his gaze back and forth between her and the tall stranger who seemed to be the cause of all that was happening to him, so that Carey found it increasingly hard to be firm. 'I'll be coming up soon, Niki,' she told him gently, but from his expression Dimitri Karamalis was impatient with such childish stubbornness and he clicked his tongue irritably.

'There is nothing to be afraid of,' he told him, and rather surprisingly Carey noticed that his voice was much less harsh than his expression. 'Katina will not harm you, she has looked after many small boys; go with her child!'

'His name is Niki!' Carey spoke up impulsively and there was a defiant angle to her chin, although she kept her voice level and as polite as possible in the circumstances. 'It's always better to use a child's name if you want to gain his confidence, Mr Karamalis.'

For a moment she thought he was going to lose his temper, and the placid-faced Katina waiting beside him looked as if she feared the outcome of such boldness. Clearly he wasn't used to being corrected, and Carey marvelled at the self-control it must have taken for him to answer as smoothly and quietly as he did.

'I concede your superior knowledge of the subject, *thespinis*, but do not presume to instruct me.'

There was tension in the lean body and an air of menace about him that showed in his eyes, sending a flutter of warning rifling along her spine, but she stuck to her guns for Niki's sake. 'Children are my job, Mr Karamalis, and I'm merely trying to ease the way. If Niki is to stay here it will make things much easier if you get along together.' She didn't wait to judge the effect of her brief lecture, but bent and kissed Niki's cheek, then took his solemn little face between her hands. 'Go with the lady, Niki, please, like a good boy, and I promise I'll come and see you very soon.'

His mouth was drawn in to stop his lip from trembling and he looked reproachfully at the new uncle he wasn't at all sure he liked, but he was a normally obedient child and he had her assurance that she would be going to see him. 'You *will* come?' he insisted, and Carey nodded.

'I'll come, I promise.'

He looked up warily when the woman reached for his hand, but she was kindly-looking and she smiled, so he put his hand in hers and walked off with her. There was something so incredibly touching about his small, straight-backed figure walking across the great hall that Carey brushed a hasty hand across her eyes.

'You are fond of him?'

Not only the question surprised her, but also an un-expected softness in the deep and rather attractive voice, and Carey turned quickly and looked at him for a moment before she answered. 'For four years I've been more like his mother than his nurse,' she said huskily. 'I've given him his meals, seen him off to school since he's been going, and loved and scolded him when he's needed it. I—I know I shouldn't have allowed myself to grow so attached to him, but he's an affectionate child and it isn't always easy to keep to the rules.'

'And you like children.'

The statement was the first approving thing he had said to her, and it took her by surprise, just as his question about Niki had. 'Naturally I like children, Mr Karamalis, it's why I became a children's nurse. But there are certain rules one is supposed to abide by, and not becoming too emotionally involved with the child is one of them. I—I suppose it's because Niki is my first charge that it's happened, and now that——' She swallowed hastily be-cause the spectre of the inevitable parting was looming up again, but it was completely unexpected when she looked up and saw compassion in the watching black eyes. 'I'm sorry,' she whispered a little breathlessly, but Dimitri Karamalis was shaking his head.

'I am sure you will feel better when you have refreshed yourself,' he said, smoothing over her embarrassment. 'Loukia will show you to your room.'

'Thank you.' She was uncertain of him in this more benevolent mood, and she suddenly recalled his brother's remarks about his having planned for her to stay. 'I hope you haven't gone to too much trouble on my account, Mr Karamalis; as I told Mr—your brother, I can find a room somewhere for the very short time I shall be here.'

'There is no need.'

'It's very good of you, but I shall be leaving again very soon.'

His eyes narrowed slightly and again Carey realised how much he resented being opposed, however mildly. 'That has yet to be decided,' he informed her.

'Oh, there's no question about it,' Carey insisted. 'Much as I hate to leave Niki, the longer I'm around the less likely he is to settle down and the harder it will be when we *do* have to part. But it isn't only that, I have to get back to England and find myself another job.'

Her heart was rapping hard at her ribs at the mere thought of it, but Dimitri Karamalis merely shrugged. 'It will be more convenient to have you here until we see how matters work out,' he declared firmly. 'And now, Miss Gordon, please allow Loukia to show you to your room. Excuse me.'

He made a signal to the waiting girl and she started forward, but Carey wasn't to be so easily forced into a situation that was none of her choosing. 'Just a minute,' she called after him, but he merely half-turned his head and somehow contrived to make it a slight bow at the same time.

'Excuse me, *thespinis*!'

It was useless, Carey thought ruefully, as she watched the departing back, for he recognised no opinion but his own. Whatever she had expected when she left England to find Aliki's brother it had not been what amounted to an order to stay there until he chose to let her go. And as much as she had seen of Dimitri Karamalis so far had not convinced her that he was the right guardian for Niki; but perhaps in the circumstances it might be better for her to stay on as he said, just to make sure all went well for Niki. As long as she could cope with his uncle.

Carey was accustomed to good living, but the luxury of her present surroundings was far and above anything she had ever dreamed of. The bedroom she had been given was big and airy and bright with reflected sunlight, while green shutters kept the worst of the heat at bay, and two tall windows gave a green and peaceful view of vine-clad hillsides. Talking to Aliki she had realised that the Karamalis family were wealthy, but she had never imagined such extravagant luxury as this.

There was a bathroom adjoining her bedroom, and that too was like nothing she had ever seen before. A dream in pink marble and gilt mirrors, and white fur carpet to step on to when she got out of her bath, so that putting on even the best dress she had available seemed like an anti-climax. Her choice was limited, for she didn't anticipate staying more than a day or two, whatever Dimitri Karamalis said to the contrary.

Having bathed and changed she then went in search of Niki and found him fast asleep in a room just as big as the one she had been given. He had presumably been given the promised meal and she could see no sign of tears having been shed; the fact that he had settled down to sleep was a good sign, she told herself, and a young girl had been left on watch in his room which showed that someone cared.

As she made her way towards the stairs she wasn't look-ing forward to the forthcoming confrontation with Aliki's family that Dimitri Karamalis had warned her would take place when the evening meal was finished. But she supposed the interview was inevitable, since he had decreed it, for he was a man who would brook no differ-ence of opinion, she guessed, and wondered just how the rest of the family regarded him. Mitso, his youngest brother, obviously had a healthy respect for his authority, but she thought there was affection there too.

Looking down into the hall from the top of the stairs, she realised just how many doors there were leading off it, and she had no idea which one she wanted. She had never felt so sickeningly nervous in her life before, and she kept a firm hold on the cool marble baluster rail as she came down the stairs, those wide elegant stairs that made her feel she was making an entrance.

Under the lights that now lit the vast hall like a stage

set her fair hair appeared even lighter, and her skin took on a creamy glow that was flattered by the blue dress she was wearing. It was sleeveless and showed a discreet amount of neck and shoulders, but it looked very plain and simple in her present surroundings. She had nothing more extravagant with her and she hoped it wouldn't be too noticeably out of place, but it caused another small niggling anxiety as she came downstairs.

'Ah, Miss Gordon!'

It annoyed her that she started so nervously when Dimitri Karamalis came out from one of the rooms, looking rather pointedly at his wristwatch, and the sudden more rapid beat of her heart she put down to the sheer overbearing presence of the man. He came no farther than just outside the door, and it was a quite unconscious gesture of defiance when Carey strolled across to him instead of hurrying as he obviously expected her to.

'Have I been too long?' she asked, her voice husky and slightly breathless. 'I had a bath and changed and then looked in on Niki; he was fast asleep.'

'He was very tired,' she was informed, as if she didn't know, 'and Katina is very good with children.'

Thankful as she was for Niki's sake that he had settled in so well, she had been slightly put out to find he had gone straight off to sleep without waiting for her to fulfil her promise to go and see him, and something of how she felt probably showed in her face. 'I'm glad for his sake,' she said, and noticed how one black brow was quickly arched for a moment.

'But you are disappointed that he did not stay awake to see you,' Dimitri Karamalis suggested. Then, giving her no time to deny it, he made an impatient sign with his hand that she automatically obeyed with a brisker step. 'Come!'

In order to open the door for her he had to lean past her, and the inevitable contact with a stunningly masculine body had such an effect on her senses that Carey caught her breath and would have drawn back, had she had room. A brief upward glance showed a look in his eyes that seemed to mock her wariness of him and brought a flood of colour to her cheeks at just the moment when she wanted to appear most self-possessed.

He followed immediately behind her, and the unexpected touch of his hand under her elbow as he guided her forward added to her discomfort, for he was a disturbing enough escort without the added sensation of physical contact. Her first glimpse of the four other women in the room brought home to her just how plain and simple her own dress was, for they were like richly plumaged peacocks in silk dresses and extravagant jewellery.

As if he read her desire to slip away again, Dimitri's light touch briefly increased its pressure. 'Do not be so nervous,' he admonished. 'There is no need for it.'

Unable to agree with him, Carey took refuge in taking stock of her surroundings as they crossed the big room, and found it as impressive as the rest of the villa that she had seen so far. It was square and high-ceilinged and almost dazzlingly bright, thanks to a dozen or so crystal lamps that hung from the ceiling and shone with the brilliance of diamonds, casting rainbow reflections on the white surfaces of walls and ceiling.

She had no time to take note of the sumptuous furnishings as she walked the last few feet on trembling legs, and only Dimitri kept her going. She felt very small and dismayingly insignificant as she was presented to an elderly woman who sat in a low, cushioned armchair surrounded by the rest of the company, for there was something almost regal about her.

'Madame Karamalis, my mother,' Dimitri's deep voice pronounced discomfitingly close to her ear, and Carey took the proffered hand warily for it seemed so bony and fragile she feared it might break.

The eyes were deep-set and as black as her eldest son's, but they were kindly enough to pity her nervousness and to Carey that meant a lot. 'Miss Gordon, we are pleased to welcome you, both as a visitor to our country and as the guardian of my grandson, Nikolas. *Kalós írthate, kalós orísate.*'

Her accent was very strong, almost unintelligible to Carey, but it was her genuine welcome that she judged her by, and she believed the old lady truly did welcome her. It was a good beginning, she felt, and moved on to the next introduction with a little more confidence, that guiding hand still hovering close to her elbow.

The man standing immediately behind the old lady was tall and dark and very much like Mitso, so that Carey had little difficulty in guessing he was the third brother. 'My brother, Andoni.' A brief handshake was all there was time for in that instance, 'and his wife Rhoda.'

Rhoda Karamalis was a little taller than Carey and slenderly dark, but despite the smile she summoned there was a suggestion of discontent in the thrust of a full lower lip, Carey thought, and for the first time paused to wonder what kind of husbands the Karamalis made. So far Andoni was the only one who she knew for certain was married, and she viewed the other two women with more interest because of it, for it occurred to her that one of them might be Dimitri's wife. Aliki had been so long out of touch with her family that she had no idea of how many of them were married and had families.

Beside Rhoda Karamalis stood a tall thin woman who watched the proceedings with black, vigilant eyes. 'My sister, Minerva Thoulou,' Dimitri introduced her, and Carey recalled vaguely that Aliki had mentioned a widowed sister who had lost her husband only months after her marriage and never fully recovered from the loss.

Because she remembered, Carey gave her a shy smile of sympathy, but the gesture went unheeded; it made no impression at all on the brooding unhappiness of the woman's features. In fact it struck her that so far as she could see Mitso was the only one of the Karamalis who appeared even the least bit lighthearted, and he was standing at the end of the group watching her with those bold, expressive eyes of his and his mouth touched by a hint of a smile.

Next to Minerva was a boy of about fifteen who was keeping his eyes downcast at the moment. 'My nephew, Damon Karamalis,' Dimitri told her. He was handsome in the Karamalis tradition, but he regarded Carey with a glowering look of resentment as he shook her hand, and she could not imagine what she had done to deserve it. She was aware of his broodingly dark eyes following her as she moved along to be introduced to the only remaining female.

The girl facing her was about her own age and quite a beauty in the same sultry, voluptuous way that Aliki had been. She had an olive skin and dark, heavily-fringed eyes and a full mouth that made no pretence of smiling. She shook hands firmly enough, but held Carey's gaze all the time and then very deliberately glanced from the corner of her eyes at Mitso standing next to her.

'And Despina Glezos, who is the fiancée of my brother Mitso.'

So the bold and flirtatious Mitso had a fiancée, which explained that knowing, sidelong look. Any girl who became engaged to someone like Mitso Karamalis would need to know exactly what she was doing, and Despina Glezos had left Carey in little doubt that she knew he had been flirting with her.

Dimitri apparently was unattached, or else he was a widower, and it surprised Carey to realise just how interested she was to know which it was. She glanced up at him when she felt herself the centre of everyone's interest and surprised by a slight smile on that dark, stern face that was strangely reassuring in the circumstances.

'Now that is over we can have dinner,' he said, and again touched her arm lightly with his fingertips, urging her forward when he moved to help his mother from her chair.

He was accustomed to taking charge, Carey guessed as she obediently went with him, and noticed the look he gave Mitso in the hope of quelling a rashly bold smile he gave her, regardless of his fiancée clinging to his arm. His eyes showed a hint of defiance for a moment and it wasn't hard to guess that there would be frequent clashes between the two of them. Nevertheless the smile disappeared, and Mitso glanced briefly and sheepishly at Despina Glezos holding tightly to his arm.

'Please consider yourself a welcome guest in our house, Miss Gordon.'

Carey looked up quickly, startled for a moment, then convinced that the words were not meant literally, but were simply a polite ritual accorded to a guest. Nevertheless they gave her food for thought as they went into dinner, for she had not anticipated becoming quite so involved. A short interview with Dimitri concerning Niki had been as much as she expected, but not being introduced to the whole family, and regarded in the dark, wary way that the Karamalis regarded her.

Walking beside Dimitri she was again conscious of the incredible sensuality of the man, and the lightness of his fingertips under her arm increased the beat of her heart alarmingly, as well as bringing a flush to her cheeks. She could cope with someone like Mitso who was, in his own way, quite open and obvious, but Dimitri was another matter altogether, and his effect on her was disturbing to say the least.

'After dinner my mother and I would like to speak to you about Aliki.' The smoothly deep voice broke in on her thoughts and Carey glanced up at him swiftly, vaguely uncertain of what he had said. 'And you have not the slightest need to look so alarmed, *thespinis*,' he went on, 'no one has the least wish to do you harm.'

'No, of course not.'

She was momentarily distracted by the room they came into, for it was even brighter and more dazzling than the *salon* they had just left. A long dark table ran the whole of the length of the room and was set with bowls of scented flowers as well as the richness of silver and snowy white linen, and wine glasses that winked and shone like diamonds. It was beautiful and quite breathtaking.

Madame Karamalis was seated reverently at the head of the table, and Carey part way along, but before he saw her seated Dimitri leaned and murmured almost in her ear, what could only have been taken as a warning. 'One matter I must insist upon, Miss Gordon, is that you do not accept an invitation to walk in the garden with my brother Mitso.'

'Well, of course I won't!' Her indignation was automatic, particularly as Mitso was at that moment seeing his fiancée seated at the table. 'With Miss Glezos on hand he's very unlikely to ask me, surely!'

Heavy-lidded eyes mocked her innocence in such matters and there was a faint curl to his upper lip that was not quite a smile. 'Allow me to know my brother, *thespinís*; the temptation of a pretty young woman will prove irresistible to him, and it is because I *know* he will ask you that I insist you refuse!'

'You can count on it!'

He pushed in her chair and just for a moment as he drew back, his long brown hands brushed her shoulders and made her shiver. 'I *will* count on it, *thespinís!*' With that he walked off, leaving Carey to wonder at the sheer arrogance of the man. She could never like him, she was convinced, but she couldn't ignore him either.

CHAPTER TWO

IT was purely and simply habit to go and check on Niki during the evening, and Carey thought no one noticed her slip away while the Karamalis family moved back from the dining-room to the *salon* after dinner. There was a great deal of conversation, all of it Greek, and they seemed to be pretty well absorbed with their own affairs, so that she didn't anticipate anyone noticing her go.

She realised her mistake when she was about half-way across the hall and she heard footsteps coming after her. So certain was she that it would be Dimitri that when she turned she had an explanation already half formed. But it wasn't Dimitri, it was Mitso, and the way he looked made her realise that his brother had been right about him. His dark eyes glowed with speculation and mischief, and she recognised that blandly confident smile as typical of him.

'You are not running away, are you?' he asked, and Carey shook her head.

'No, Mr Karamalis, I'm just going upstairs to check on Niki as I do every evening about this time.'

His mouth pursed derisively and one shoulder lifted in a careless shrug, and not for a moment did he anticipate any opposition. 'There is no need for you to do that this evening,' he told her, 'there will be someone to see that he is well cared for. I have a much more attractive proposition; outside the gardens are beautiful and the Greek moon is like no other in the world, Miss Gordon, I swear to you!'

He was temptation, Carey recognised, and almost irresistible, but she still had his brother's warning in mind; no one in their right mind would deliberately defy Dimitri Karamalis, whatever the temptation. Also Mitso had a fiancée, and she surely had to be taken into account. 'I'm

sure it's every bit as beautiful as you say, Mr Karamalis,'
she said firmly, 'but I still can't come with you. When
I've checked on Niki I have—a kind of appointment to
see your brother and Madame Karamalis.'

'To tell them about Aliki—yes, I know.' Mitso dismissed
her reasons with a scornful hand and the slight thrust of
his bottom lip suggested that he was not accustomed to
being turned down. 'But no one is looking for you right at
this moment, and when Dimitri wishes to see you he will
know where to find you.'

'That's exactly my point,' Carey told him with a faint
smile. 'He warned me before dinner that you were likely
to suggest a walk in the garden afterwards and I assured
him I wouldn't go with you. Besides, wasn't I told that
you were engaged to Miss Glezos?'

He shrugged carelessly, but his mouth had a definitely
sulky look and he obviously didn't like being reminded of
where his attention belonged. 'Despina will not mind.'

'Maybe not,' said Carey, wondering how often he had
said that in the past, 'but I do, Mr Karamalis.'

'My name is Mitso!' He was determined to have one thing
go in his favour, and his dark eyes showed just how much he
resented being turned down. 'Unless you are determined to
be unfriendly, why do you not use my first name? Surely
Dimitri has not forbidden you to do that too!'

He was hitting back and uncaring what he said, and he
was very nearly as strong-willed as Dimitri, though much
less awesome. 'No one has forbidden me to do anything,
Mr Karamalis,' she told him with studied quietness, 'but I
think it's much better to keep things on a more formal
footing at the moment. Strictly speaking I'm not really a
guest. I'm an ex-employee of your sister's and I'm quite
sure Mr Dimitri Karamalis would rather I didn't get too
familiar with you.'

Her calmness, assumed or not, seemed to annoy him,
and Mitso curled his lip while his eyes mocked her concern
for Dimitri's opinion. 'I had not realised that you were

afraid of Dimitri,' he told her, and Carey flushed in such a way that he must have known she wasn't telling the truth when she denied it.

'Nothing of the kind! I simply don't want any trouble during the short time I'm here, that's all. I want everything to go as smoothly as possible for Niki's sake.'

'For Niki's sake!' His eyes gleamed mockingly at her. 'Do you think it can—go smoothly? Until now Damon has been the only grandchild and has been doted on by his grandmother, do you think that Damon will welcome another grandson with whom he will have to share her love? Do you think Andoni and Rhoda will welcome another Karamalis to share in the family business?'

'And you, Mr Karamalis?' Carey asked impulsively. 'How do you feel about Niki—your sister's child?'

Thick black lashes hid his eyes for a moment and the expression on his face was hard to interpret. 'He is Aliki's child,' he said after a moment or two, 'and he is a Karamalis, therefore he belongs here. I feel as Dimitri does, that it is his place.'

It is his place. No more, just the plain fact that as a Karamalis Niki belonged with them whatever the circumstances of his birth. Not a word about/him being loved or wanted, just that he belonged there; only the recollection of a certain gentle look in Madame Karamalis's eyes stopped Carey from fetching Niki and leaving there and then. To someone who loved Niki as much as she did, it was hard to understand the attitude of Aliki's family as defined by Mitso.

There was a lump in her throat and she clasped her hands tightly together, determinedly cool as she faced Mitso's dark, speculative gaze. 'If you'll excuse me,' she said, 'I'll go and see that Niki is all right before I'm wanted elsewhere.'

'You will not come with me?'

Carey shook her head. He found it very hard to accept, she thought, but she was firm and moved away from him even before she had finished speaking. 'No, I'm sorry, Mr Karamalis, it's better that I don't, and I really don't have the time.'

He said something harsh and virulent in Greek and turned swiftly to go striding across the hall and up the stairs, taking the steps two at a time. Evidently the attractions of the garden were less alluring without her company, and she wondered why on earth the sultry Despina Glezos put up with his roving eye. She didn't fool herself that she was the first pretty girl he had flirted with, and nor would she be the last, for men like Mitso Karamalis were dangerously attractive and made the most of their charm and good looks. But she could cope with him for the brief time she was to be there, she felt sure; and if she did find herself slipping Dimitri would be there to remind her.

It took no more than a few minutes to check on Niki, and she found him still sleeping soundly. There was no sign of the girl who had been sitting with him when she paid her earlier visit, but Niki appeared to be in a deep and peaceful sleep and, although she was thankful for his sake, she again felt a little twinge of disappointment because he had not managed to stay awake for her goodnight kiss.

She heard the hum of voices in the *salon* as she came downstairs again, but no one appeared to be waiting for her to come down, so presumably she was not wanted for the dreaded interview yet, and she was tempted to take advantage of the free moment. She had turned down Mitso's invitation, but the idea of walking in the garden for a few minutes was an attractive one, and with a quick glance at the *salon* door she hurried across the hall and out into the garden.

Mitso had been right. It was very very beautiful, and the Greek moon did seem bigger and more mellow than any she had seen before, giving an even more exotic effect to the flowers and shrubs that filled the night air with their scent. How could she not respond to the dark sweep of cypress plumes against a deep purple sky, or the rustle of orange and lemon trees spreading their perfume on the night wind?

It was all so incredibly lovely that just for a moment she wished she might stay there with Niki, and as she moved slowly along the moonlit path she felt a sense of peace and pleasure she had never known before. Greece was a magic land, as Aliki had so often claimed, and she would find it all too easy to fall under its spell if she didn't remind herself why she was there and how little time she had to enjoy it.

It was the faint but definite clip of footsteps on the stone-paved path that brought her swiftly back to earth, and she caught her breath audibly when a tall, shadowy figure appeared just ahead of her, looming out of the moonlit garden like a menacing ghost. But no ghost possessed such fierce black eyes that sent small shivers chasing one another up and down her spine, and it was a man of flesh and blood who made her pulse pound so hard that it almost deafened her.

His complexion seemed to be nearly black in the shimmering moonlight and every strong feature was etched with deep shadows that gave him an alarming look of malevolence. Dimitri was obviously angry, but at the moment Carey could not imagine why, for he surely could not object to her walking in the gardens.

'So,' he said, as she came nearer, 'you found my brother's invitation too much to resist after all, *thespinís*!'

Carey wished he wouldn't use that very formal title as if it was a term of abuse, and she flushed at the very idea of his suggesting she had gone with Mitso after all. She couldn't really blame him for not trusting his brother; he obviously had reason, but she resented him accusing her. 'I last saw your brother going upstairs in a huff because I wouldn't go for a walk in the garden with him, Mr Karamalis,' she told him. 'And I resent your assumption that I would automatically do exactly as you asked me not to!'

'But he came out of the *salon* after you,' he insisted.

'I've already said he did!' Carey was keeping a very firm hold on her temper, for no man had ever got under her skin the way Dimitri Karamalis did. 'In fact I've been walking on my own,' she went on, 'I needed some fresh air and a moment or two on my own to think. I should have come out here even if Mr—your brother hadn't made it sound so heavenly, but I had no intention of coming with him, and I told him so!'

It was strange why she felt so curiously lightheaded and excited for this man was unlikely to have the same motives as his younger brother for coming after her. Yet her whole body was trembling and her heart was beating so hard and fast that it was making her head spin, and it had to be because of Dimitri Karamalis.

He was as lean as a big cat, and looked every bit as dangerous as he stood there judging her with those narrowed black eyes, the snowy whiteness of his dress shirt in stunning contrast to his dark features. He seemed so much taller too, and the air of threat about him stirred a responsive shiver in the most primitive depths of her soul.

'It seems,' he said, 'that I must congratulate you on your powers of resistance!'

Flushed and trembling and with a defiant angle to her chin, Carey looked up at him again. 'It wasn't very hard when I took Miss Glezos into account,' she told him. 'In her place I'd be furious if I saw my fiancé follow a strange woman out of the room with the obvious intention of seducing her!'

He said nothing for several moments and if Carey could have slipped past him she would have done, but he completely barred her way and it was doubtful if she could have got past without coming into close contact with him; the last thing she wanted. Instead those black eyes watched her with an intent steadiness that made every nerve in her body flutter in response, and she lowered her eyes at last.

In the sleeveless blue dress she looked and felt very

small and rather exposed, her fair hair lightened to almost silver in the moonlight, and her grey eyes shadowed to a darkness almost as deep as his. 'You are not what I expected,' he declared, and the observation startled her so much that Carey stared up at him for a moment without saying anything.

Then she shook her head. 'I can't imagine what you did expect, Mr Karamalis,' she said in a slightly husky voice. 'I explained in my letter that I was looking after Niki; that I was his nanny.'

'I did not expect anyone so young or so lovely,' he explained smoothly, and the soft, deep voice touched her like a caress, making her shake her head slowly to dispel its effect. 'In fact, Miss Gordon, I expected something much more like the traditional English nanny one hears so much about. A stout and middle-aged woman dressed in sensible shoes and a dark uniform.'

'That's a very old-fashioned view!'

'So it seems.' A slight nod conceded her superior knowledge, but she was beginning to find the continued scrutiny infinitely disturbing. If only he would move, just slightly, she might manage to slip past him, but he remained where he was, firmly ensconced in a bold arrogant stance directly in her path. 'You do not dislike Greece, Miss Gordon?'

His tone suggested that the question was superfluous, for no Greek could visualise anyone not liking his country, and Carey's nod was almost automatic. 'I've seen very little of it,' she confessed. 'Only the drive from Athens to here, but it looks lovely once the suburbs are left behind.'

'Then you should settle in quickly.' She would have said that she had no intention of settling in as she had only a few days before she must go back and see about another post, but she was given no opportunity to say a single word. 'If you will write a covering letter giving permission for the rest of your things to be picked up,' he went on, 'I will see to it that they are put on the first available transport.'

Carey was staring at him, for it was impossible she had misunderstood. His brother had intimated that Dimitri had it all arranged, but she had not anticipated anything quite so final as he was making it sound. 'I have all I need with me, Mr Karamalis,' she told him. 'I'm here for only a few days, so I don't need very much. Just until Niki settles in.'

But quite clearly she need not have bothered saying anything, for he was taking no notice at all of her intentions, merely stating his own. Standing as he was with his head held back, the moonlight exaggerated the deep cleft in his chin, and the high, almost oriental curve of the cheekbones, thick lashes casting shadows over the gleaming blackness of his eyes.

'I would prefer that you remain for longer,' he told her, 'and I shall make arrangements accordingly, Miss Gordon. Do you have relatives you will need to inform?'

Rather dazedly Carey shook her head. She had no intention of being bulldozed into something she hadn't planned and wasn't sure she wanted, although she could not claim that she actually wanted to part from Niki, but she seemed to be whisked along without any chance to make her own wishes heard. 'There's no one,' she said. 'But——'

'Good, then that will make it rather easier. You find your room quite comfortable?'

'Very, but I really have no intention of staying for long, Mr Karamalis, I thought you understood that.'

'I understood that you had been in charge of my nephew for some time now, and I wish the arrangement to continue.'

There was a curiously taut sensation in her stomach and her heart was thudding hard with mingled excitement and confusion. 'But why?' she asked. 'There's simply no point in my staying too long. The longer I'm around the harder it's going to be for Niki when I go—it would simply prolong the agony.'

'I disagree!'

It was virtually impossible to get anything across to this man, Carey thought wildly. He just wasn't interested in any plans but his own and he was determined she was going to stay, although she could not at the moment see why he was so set on it. Aliki had had a certain streak of stubbornness, but nothing to compare with this brother of hers.

'Come, Miss Gordon,' he said impatiently, 'you have already said that you like what you have seen of Greece so far, so why do you so dislike the idea of remaining here for longer than you had planned?'

'I've told you, it will be harder for Niki——'

'And I have said that I disagree. When Nikolas has settled in and feels at home here, then it will be a better time for you to go, you must surely see the sense of that.'

Carey's brain was spinning and she had to recognise that she was tempted, she couldn't deny it, though whether she agreed with his reasoning she wasn't so sure. 'I don't know about that,' she demurred, but once more he took it upon himself to assure her.

'It is common sense, Miss Gordon, both from Nikolas's point of view and yours. You say you have no family ties to call you back, and you will, I imagine, be seeking other employment when you return, so there is no credible reason why you should not remain here for the time being. You will act in the same capacity as my sister employed you, for a salary to be agreed, I see no reason for your objection.'

Dazed and on the point of yielding, Carey shook her head. 'I—I was under the impression that Niki was to learn to speak Greek,' she began. 'If I stay——'

'Still you put obstacles in the way,' Dimitri remarked, 'and I cannot see why you do, Miss Gordon. If you are fond of him you surely wish to remain with Nikolas as long as possible. Or perhaps you fear you cannot get along with the other members of my family and therefore cannot face living under the same roof with them?'

'Nothing of the kind,' Carey denied hastily.

He was so determined, and in her heart she was quite happy to stay, as long as it didn't make things even harder when the time came. But there were certain things that made her see drawbacks as well, like the dark gleam in Mitso Karamalis's eyes when he looked at her. Tempting and speculating, and waiting for her to weaken, because sooner or later women must always weaken with a man like Mitso Karamalis.

'In that case I will contact our London office and have your things sent on,' he informed her, and Carey was startled into remarking on something quite unexpected.

Aliki had never once mentioned that her family had an office in London, and she surely would have done had she known of it. 'You have a London office?' she asked, and Dimitri narrowed his eyes slightly.

'A recent acquisition that my sister would not have known about,' he said, and glanced at his wristwatch as if the passage of time was of importance to him. 'And now, Miss Gordon, perhaps you are ready to talk to us about Aliki?'

So it had finally come to it. Carey looked up at that dark, implacable face and hesitated, making no secret of her reluctance. Not that there was likely to be any alternative, she guessed, not with Dimitri Karamalis taking a hand. 'If I must,' she told him, 'but to be quite honest, Mr Karamalis, I don't really like the idea of talking about her now she's gone.'

'Now she has gone.' He echoed the phrase so softly that she felt a slight flutter over her skin, as if her senses were touched by something in his voice. 'Do you not understand, Miss Gordon,' he went on, 'that it is because she is gone and we shall never now have the opportunity of— making up, that we have such a need to know what happened to her during those years she was away from us?'

Aliki had been possessed of the same pride, and she

would probably have understood, but Carey found it harder to imagine this grand and autocratic family regretting their treatment of her. Madame Karamalis, perhaps, and possibly Mitso too, might have been ready to forgot and forgive, but on the whole she could not imagine them apologising for anything they did. And particularly not Dimitri.

'I suppose so,' she allowed after a moment or two, and noticed how he frowned.

'Come, Miss Gordon, have you never done something that you regret, and been unable to bring yourself to back down?' he demanded in a voice that was more harsh than she had heard it so far. 'If you have not you are very fortunate!'

Never having been involved in anything as emotionally shattering as a family quarrel, Carey found it hard to put herself in their place, but eventually she thought she could see the dilemma they must have been in. It would be very hard for anyone in this proud and arrogant family to unbend enough to make the first move, but that did not mean they were not inwardly as hurt as Aliki herself had been.

'I think I understand,' she ventured, glancing briefly at Dimitri's strong, unyielding features. 'I think—I sometimes felt that Aliki wanted to make up, to write and ask your forgiveness, but she couldn't bring herself to it.'

'She was a Karamalis,' Dimitri observed quietly. 'It would not be easy.'

Carey said nothing for the moment, but she felt she had at last caught a glimpse of the real people behind that barrier of pride that made them so unapproachable, and she did not envy them one bit. It seemed almost an unconscious gesture when long fingers brushed lightly on her arm, and she looked up quickly to see Dimitri standing aside, inviting her to walk alongside him, back to the house.

'You brought us Aliki's son,' he said, in that same quiet

and infinitely affecting voice. 'You can tell us more about her than anyone—except perhaps her lover.'

'I won't talk about him!'

It was a quick, instinctive response and she knew it was bound to have his attention. 'You did not like him?' Dimitri asked, and Carey bit anxiously on her lip for a moment before she replied.

'He didn't even go and see her in hospital when she was dying,' she said in a small husky voice that suggested the hurt had been as much hers as Aliki's. 'He didn't want to see Niki; he didn't even come and ask what was going to happen to him. He simply didn't care!'

'And you hate him for it?'

'I hate him for it!' she confirmed chokingly. 'I liked Aliki, whatever she'd done, and I love Niki; I couldn't imagine any man simply abandoning them both as if they didn't exist!'

'You have talked about him,' Dimitri pointed out quietly, and just for a second his fingers pressed hard into her flesh. 'There will be no more need for you to mention him; I know how you feel and for my sister's sake I appreciate it.'

Shaken by the accustomed emotion, Carey said nothing, but she was very much aware of the man beside her as they walked back to the house together. His hand still lightly supported her arm and brought a fluttering urgency to her pulse, and there was a stunning aura of maleness about him that she could not ignore or be unaffected by. If she *was* to stay on at the Villa Karamalis it would not only be Mitso who presented a problem, and her reaction to Dimitri could prove much more difficult to cope with.

When Carey woke the next morning there was an un-accustomed churning of excitement in her stomach that it took her a moment or two to find a reason for. Then she recalled that she had more or less been shanghaied into remaining there, for as long as Dimitri Karamalis considered necessary, presumably.

She could see that it made sense, now that she had thought about it, because in fact Niki was going to be much less troubled about her leaving him when he was settled happily into his new family. Much less so than if she had gone off after only a couple of days and left him in a strange environment among a lot of strangers. Dimitri was right.

She pulled a face as she got out of bed, wondering how often Dimitri was proved right, and if that was what made him so confident of his own opinions. When she walked over and looked out of the window, the sun was brilliant with not a cloud in the clear blue sky, while in the distance, but not too far away, was a glimpse of white columns on a wooded hillside. It was true, she decided, that Greece had a magic of its own, but she wondered how much opportunity she would have to see more of it, and who would be her guide if she did.

She had no idea what plans had been made for Niki. Whether he was to go to school, or be taught at home, she didn't know, but no doubt Dimitri would soon enlighten her. That the decision would be Dimitri's she had no doubt at all, for he was the recognised head of the family, and he was not the kind of man to delegate his authority.

The pale yellow dress she had on this morning gave her a rather ethereal look combined with her pale skin and light hair, and she studied her reflection thoughtfully for a moment before she went along to Niki's room. She both looked and felt very alien among these dark, proud Greeks, but she had never been afraid of a challenge, and that was what her stay there could well prove to be.

With a sigh for what was likely to come, she left her room and went along to Niki's, stopping short outside the door when she heard the unmistakable sound of his laughter. She hesitated because it was so completely unexpected and, although she knew she should be glad to hear it, just for a moment it gave her a curious feeling of isolation.

When she opened the door she found the same young girl who had sat with him the night before. She was no more than fifteen or sixteen and their laughter was the laughter of children, as the girl tried in vain to brush some semblance of order into Niki's thick black curls. She looked up quickly when the door opened, and seemed to be expecting a scolding, but instead Carey smiled at her.

'*Kaliméra, thespinís,*' she murmured, and ducked quickly out of the room.

As the door closed behind her, Carey turned to look at Niki and found him in possession of the hairbrush and doing his best to brush his own hair. 'Irene is nice,' he announced as she took the brush from him. 'Carey, she thought I was too small to dress myself, but I showed her!'

Obviously he had enjoyed the interlude for he was still smiling broadly, and Carey gave him a speculative look via the dressing-table mirror. 'You're getting so independent that you soon won't need anyone to help you, will you?' she asked, but from the way he looked that aspect hadn't occurred to him.

'I can't brush my hair,' he pointed out after a moment or two, and when she hugged him suddenly it was because Carey felt he was letting her know he still needed her, even if it was only to brush his hair for him.

'You like it here, Niki?'

The face he pulled suggested that he needed to give it some thought, and he looked at her reflected face in the mirror. 'Are you going to stay too, Carey?'

Concentrating on what she was doing rather than look at him, Carey nodded. 'For the moment,' she told him.

'Not for ever?'

'Not for ever,' she agreed quietly. 'This isn't my home, Niki, but it is yours. This is where your mummy lived when she was a little girl, and now you're going to live here.'

'Who with?' he wanted to know, and Carey debated

the wisdom of listing all the relations he was going to meet
very soon now.

'Oh, a grandmother, uncles, aunts and a cousin.'

'All those,' Niki said, and obviously wasn't too happy
about it, so that she hastened to reassure him.

'Not so many really, darling, and you met two of your
uncles last night, do you remember?'

His frown was disturbingly like Dimitri's, she realised,
and wondered if she shouldn't be thankful that he had at
least something in common with his formidable family.
'They didn't like me much,' he observed.

'Oh, nonsense, of course they did!'

'Not that big one,' Niki insisted. 'He looked fierce at
me.'

Carey thought she could see why he described Dimitri
as the big one, even though his height was much the same
as Mitso's. That impressive bearing of his made him seem
much taller, and he had frowned at Niki, she couldn't
deny it. Trying to pave the way, she found herself making
excuses for Dimitri's seeming lack of understanding.

'Uncle Dimitri doesn't know very much about little
boys,' she said, 'that's probably why he seemed a bit—a
bit stern. But he didn't dislike you, Niki, in fact he loves
you, and he hopes you're going to live here always.'

'He does?'

Niki was always ready to like someone if they showed
the slightest hint of friendliness, and he was looking at her
hopefully. 'Of course he does,' she assured him, and prayed
she was right, and that Dimitri Karamalis was capable of
loving a small boy who had a desperate need of love.
Putting down the hairbrush, she brought herself down to
his level and took his solemn little face between her hands
for a moment before she kissed him. 'Now let's go and
meet them all, and see what's for breakfast, shall we, darling? We don't want to keep them waiting, and I'm sure
you want your breakfast, don't you?'

But breakfast was rather less important to him this

morning, Carey realised, and the laughter was gone, leaving him sober and solemn-eyed. He held tightly to her hand going downstairs, and looked around the vast hall as if he hadn't seen it before. 'They're not here,' he whispered, overawed by the size of the place, but Carey shook her head.

As they reached the foot of the stairs a young man in a white jacket came in through a door at the back of the hall and, seeing them he indicated that they should use the same door. He said something in Greek and smiled, and Carey nodded her thanks, for the sound of voices suggested that the Karamalis family were following Greek custom and eating out of doors.

The voices became more distinct when they stepped out into the sunshine, and Carey led the way along a path between wide, lush flower borders, Niki dragging behind until she was virtually hauling him along. 'Niki!' She gave his hand a sharp tug and brought him up level with her, her voice edged with nervousness. 'Don't hang back, there's a good boy.'

He obeyed, but reluctantly, and his hand gripped hers even more tightly when the path opened out suddenly into a wide, tiled *patio* with a kidney-shaped swimming pool set in the middle of it. At the far end was a long table, set beneath a huge fig tree and whatever was in store for them, Carey thought she had never seen such a lovely setting for the first meal of the day.

Four of the dozen or so chairs around the table were occupied, and it was a relief to know that they were not to meet the Karamalis *en masse*. Carey's heart was hammering hard, for the long walk around the edge of the pool gave the four people at the table the opportunity of studying them without making it too obvious. Niki's hand tightened still more, and his head had dropped, his eyes downcast as he anticipated meeting his big, formidable uncle again.

What struck Carey most about them was how dark they looked, sitting there in the shade of the fig tree, and how

overwhelmingly powerful as a group. Mitso and Andoni
were both wearing light trousers and shirts, but Dimitri,
as if determined to stand apart from the others, wore
brown slacks and a tan shirt; the shirt open at the neck to
show a long slash of muscular throat and a glimpse of
black hair. A strong, powerful and infinitely disturbing
figure that made her already racing heart beat even
faster.

The warm light wind, that seemed to be unceasing night
or day, moulded the yellow dress to her body and made it
seem to fit much more closely than it did in fact, and she
was conscious of Mitso taking note of it as she came slowly
around the pool's edge. Somewhat surprisingly Andoni
Karamalis showed appreciation too, but his was more re-
strained, a mere gleam deep in his eyes which he quickly
concealed. As for Dimitri, it was impossible to judge his
opinion, for those implaccable features gave nothing
away.

Dimitri was first on his feet, followed by Andoni, but
Mitso rose with an almost insolent slowness while his eyes
watched her with a hint of mockery; as if he knew exactly
how nervous she was and relished it. Only Madame
Karamalis showed any genuine sign of welcome, and as
she sat at the far end of the table with her sons around
her, her gaze was fixed with an almost avid intensity on
her newest grandson.

'Good morning, I hope we're not late.' Carey spoke up
quickly, for she was taut with nervousness and not sure
how early or late they were.

'You are not late,' Dimitri assured her in his deep quiet
voice, and Carey was surprised to realise how soothing it
was in her present state of agitation. '*Kaliméra*, Miss
Gordon; Nikolas.'

Despite his air of insolence Mitso seemed anxious not to
be overlooked and he drew out a chair next to him, inviting her with a flourish to sit beside him. He took no notice
at all of Niki, but then Mitso was not interested in small

boys, whether or not it happened to be his nephew, and what did not interest him he ignored. In his own way, Carey supposed, he was letting her know that he forgave her for last night's rebuff, but expected her to behave with more sense this morning.

But she had already decided what she had to do, and she smiled and shook her head, murmuring a good morning to him as she walked past, and realising that Dimitri had left his place at the table and was following her to where Madame Karamalis sat. She didn't even notice how Mitso's mouth tightened and his eyes burned with anger at a second rebuff.

Madame Karamalis smiled and extended a hand. 'Kalimēra, Miss Gordon,' she said in her thick accent. 'I hope that you were comfortable?'

'Very comfortable, thank you, Madame Karamalis. I slept very well.'

'Ah, that is good!'

Having done all that good manners required of her, the old lady turned her attention once more to the small, sturdy figure of her grandson, and with a hand in the small of his back, Carey urged him forward. She had prayed all the way downstairs that he wouldn't reject his grandmother as he had his Uncle Dimitri last night, and the testing time was here.

But she need not have worried, for Niki didn't turn away nor back off, but regarded the brown wrinkled face with frank interest, as if he sensed her eagerness to love him. 'This is Nikolas, Madame Karamalis; Nikolas Dimitri. Niki, this is your grandmother, Madame Karamalis.'

Carey hoped she had no need to prompt him, but he looked touchingly solemn as he shook the hand that reached out to him, and murmured the polite words he had been taught, and there was a shimmer of tears in the old lady's eyes. Drawing him closer, she held him against her knee while she cradled his head and murmured softly in her own tongue, while her three sons looked on in silence.

What were they thinking? Carely wondered. Were they thinking of Aliki whom they had shut out for so long? And could they see her huge, beautiful eyes in her son's? Dimitri was standing just behind her while she watched the tender little scene, and her heart beat anxiously hard because she couldn't be sure what exactly he would do if Niki did not submit to the show of affection.

Again she need not have worried, for Niki had no objection to being made a fuss of. He was a naturally affectionate child as a rule and he was nothing loath to be cuddled. When Carey turned and looked over her shoulder at Dimitri, it was a purely automatic reaction born of relief, and the expression she saw in his eyes both startled and puzzled her.

There was speculation and anticipation, but mostly it was the unmistakable warmth of sympathy she recognised and it was so unexpected that she turned back quickly and tried to still the sudden violence of her heartbeat. Not for a single moment had it occurred to her that he would understand her feelings at seeing Niki give his affection so readily to someone else. It was something she had not yet fully realised herself, something she had to get accustomed to.

'You do not speak Greek, eh?' Madame Karamalis's soft voice broke into the confusion of her thoughts and she brought herself swiftly back to earth. The old lady cupped Niki's face between her hands as Carey often did and she was smiling at him fondly. 'But you will soon learn to call me Yayá, will you not, little one?'

Niki pondered thoughtfully on the new word for a moment. '*Yayá*?' he queried, and it was Dimitri's voice that answered him.

'It means grandmother, Nikolas, you will remember that, eh?'

Niki nodded, but his eyes were wary when they turned

on the tall and vaguely menacing figure of his uncle. Then
he glanced at Carey who stood between them, and she
smiled at him encouragingly. 'Of course he'll remember,
won't you, Niki?'

He nodded with more confidence this time. 'Course I'll
remember.'

'Then try it, hmm?'

He turned and looked up at the smiling, doting face of
his grandmother and suddenly gave her a big mischievous
grin. 'You're my Yayá Karamalis!'

Dimitri moved around until he stood beside Carey instead of immediately behind her. 'And will you also remember that I am called Thíos Dimitri?' he asked. 'Over
there is Thíos Andoni, and Thíos Mitso you have already
met, eh?'

There was a note of softness in his voice that surprised
Carey and inevitably Niki responded to it. He was a child
who was very sensitive to mood and atmosphere and it
seemed to him that this morning Dimitri was not quite so
stern and disapproving as he had been last night. Still
held fast in his grandmother's embrace he looked up at
Dimitri with his huge dark eyes and tipped his head a
little to one side.

'Carey says I am to live with you for ever,' he said in all
seriousness. 'Will I?'

It was also unexpected when a gleam of amusement
appeared in the blackness of Dimitri's eyes, although he
kept his face straight. 'Would you like to?' he countered,
and Niki gave it some thought, then almost inevitably
looked at Carey again.

'Carey as well?' he insisted, and Dimitri too turned his
eyes on her.

They were deep and black, and the look he gave her
was long and intense so that she coloured furiously and
hated the thought of Mitso seeing it because he would be
bound to put the wrong construction on it. 'If she wishes
to,' Dimitri said gravely, 'Carey may stay for ever too.'

CHAPTER THREE

CAREY wasn't sure what the procedure was to be, so, as near as possible, she followed her normal routine the following morning. Having bathed and dressed herself she went along to supervise Niki, then took him down to breakfast at roughly the same time as she had the day before. If the family had a routine at all it obviously varied, because she found Mitso on his own and looking oddly down in the mouth.

He sat with his chin propped on one hand, looking moody and solemn and not a little sorry for himself. He was incredibly handsome in profile and as she made her way towards him, holding Niki's hand, she felt her senses responding to the sight of him, however firmly she sought to subdue them. Then he turned his head and saw her and, just as he had yesterday, he watched her walk around the edge of the pool with that bold and insolent look in his eyes.

But outwardly his manners were impeccable, and he got up as she approached and saw her seated on the chair beside him, giving her no opportunity this morning of doing anything else. '*Kaliméra*, Miss Gordon. Did you sleep well?'

He was being very proper too, probably because he wasn't sure what sort of a reaction he was going to get after yesterday, and Carey smiled to herself. 'I slept very well, thank you, Mr Karamalis.'

She saw Niki settled on the other side of her, but all the time she was conscious of Mitso watching her. A young manservant brought coffee and fresh rolls for her and Niki, but the moment he was gone again Mitso was leaning forward with both elbows on the table and bringing himself much closer. He had obviously finished his own meal but intended staying to keep her and Niki company while they had theirs; not that he took any notice of Niki, any more than he had yesterday, he simply concentrated his attention on her.

'You still insist on being so formal?' he asked in his strongly accented but persuasively soft voice, and Carey looked at him in genuine confusion for a moment. 'You still insist on calling me Mr Karamalis,' he pointed out with a touch of impatience. 'Can you not relent and call me Mitso?'

Carey gave her attention to pouring coffee into her cup and, outwardly at least, she was only partly interested in what he said. In fact it was a situation that she thought was likely to arise frequently if she didn't do as he said, and especially now that she was destined to remain with them for a while. Mitso wasn't the sort to give up easily, and clearly he didn't like being on formal terms with pretty girls.

'I thought we'd been through this,' she said after a moment or two. 'It's rather awkward for me, Mr Karamalis, because I've agreed to stay on for a time, but I shall be doing the same job I did for Aliki. In a word, I shall be an employee, and working for Mr Dimitri Karamalis.'

'And you think that Dimitri will not allow such familiarity?'

She turned her head again briefly and looked into those boldly persuasive eyes for a moment. 'Do you?' she asked.

Mitso clasped both hands together and rested his chin on them and the thickness of his lashes made it difficult to see what was in his eyes as he answered her. 'I think you do Dimitri an injustice,' he claimed. 'He is not a—snob?—and he will not object to you using my first name if I wish it. Also I would very much like to use your most unusual name—do you have objections?'

It wasn't something she could answer easily, Carey found. She didn't mind in the least being called by her first name, Aliki had always used it, but there were more than the two of them to consider. She was not convinced by his assurance that Dimitri wouldn't mind the familiarity, and also there was always Despina Glezos to be considered, particularly as she lived under the same roof as her fiancé.

'I think Miss Glezos might have objections,' she told him after a moment or two. 'I know I wouldn't like it in her place.'

He was smiling and there was a gleam of malicious mischief in his eyes when he looked at her. Chin still supported on his hands, he pulled at his pursed lips with his thumbs. 'I am driving Despina home this morning. She has been staying here with us while her parents were in Germany, but they came back last evening and now Despina goes home, hah?'

'I see.'

It shouldn't really make any difference whether Despina Glezos was there or not, the principle was the same, but somehow it did, and Carey recognised her own weakening almost as soon as Mitso did. His eyes gleamed with laughter and he reached for her hand, squeezing her fingers and apparently oblivious of Niki's interested gaze.

'I thought that you might,' he murmured, and raised her fingers to his lips. 'Now—you will call me Mitso, yes?'

'*Uncle* Mitso,' Niki's husky little voice piped up, and Mitso scowled at him so fiercely that the boy blinked.

'Uncle is for little boys,' he was told firmly. 'Carey is not a little girl and she does not have to call me anything but just Mitso. Also,' he added with a gleam of malice, 'you should use the Greek word as your Thíos Dimitri has told you.'

Niki looked at Carey for guidance as he always did, and it was only because she felt it would be to his advantage if she agreed with Mitso that she smiled and nodded at him. 'You can say that easily enough, can't you, Niki?'

'Thíos Mitso,' Niki declared with a defiant glance at

Mitso, and Carey leaned and kissed him.

'Good boy!'

'Am I not also a good boy?' Mitso demanded, determined to dismiss the little boy from their conversation again. He tightened his hold on her hand and leaned still closer until his dark eyes were looking directly into hers. 'Carey, you will call me Mitso!'

'If you insist.'

Her voice sounded so shaky that she despaired of her own weakness, but Mitso Karamalis was something new in her experience. Less overpoweringly affecting than his eldest brother, it was true, but affecting just the same. He made her want to laugh with him and forget her present tenuous situation, and that could be a dangerous state of mind.

'I insist,' he murmured, and once more conveyed her fingers to his lips.

It was doubtful if Mitso noticed anyone coming, and Carey certainly did not until Niki gave her a sudden sharp nudge with his elbow. Then she turned quickly and saw Dimitri coming along the path beside the pool, taking long strides that Despina Glezos was having difficulty in keeping up with. Carey felt immediately guilty when she saw the other girl, whereas Mitso seemed to be quite unaffected at being caught out, as it were; arrogantly sure of himself and of his fiancée.

Despina looked older somehow this morning, and Carey wondered if it had anything to do with the fact that she was seeing her for the first time in harsh sunlight. Her black hair was pulled back and held in place by a tortoiseshell slide, and a plain cream dress that must have cost a fortune by Carey's standards showed off every luscious curve as she came hurrying towards them, her dark eyes darting between the two of them and unmistakably suspicious.

Carey drew back her hand, making the movement as inconspicuous as possible, but it was almost certain that at least one of the newcomers noticed it. Instinct made her want to get to her feet, Dimitri Karamalis had that effect on her, but instead she stayed where she was, looking at him through the thickness of her lashes when he took the chair directly opposite to her.

A shirt of quite startling whiteness showed off his dark skin, and while he sat facing her she found it easy to forget all about Mitso who, only a few moments ago, had seemed irresistible. Something about Dimitri Karamalis touched depths in her she had never known existed, and realising it both alarmed and annoyed her, for she was not accustomed to having her self-confidence undermined as he seemed able to do.

Because she needed to assert herself, she looked very deliberately at him and met his eyes with a boldness she was far from feeling. 'I don't know what plans you have for Niki this morning, Mr Karamalis. Normally he would be at school, of course, but——'

'In Greece children do not begin at primary school until they are six years old,' Dimitri informed her. 'Since Nikolas is only just that age there is time yet for arrangements to be made for him. In the meantime he is in your hands, Miss Gordon.'

'I see—thank you.'

For the moment Mitso was giving all his attention to Despina Glezos who had taken the seat on the other side of him, and they had their heads together, murmuring in their own tongue and seemingly oblivious of anyone else. It was very doubtful if they heard the quiet words that Dimitri said to Carey as he leaned across the table towards her, his black eyes fixed on her steadily so that she was pretty sure he was going to start a discussion of some kind, and swallowed anxiously.

'If you were in the place of Despina Glezos, Miss Gordon, would you be happy to discover your fiancé flirting with another woman at the breakfast table?'

Carey flushed, and for a moment was at a loss for words,

for she couldn't deny the situation he described. Mitso
had not only been holding hands with her, he had been
kissing her fingers, and her hope that neither of the newcomers had noticed was in vain. Very little escaped
Dimitri's eagle eye. 'It wasn't the way it looked,' she
insisted, but the black gaze was unwavering.

'My brother was holding your hand and you were not,
that I noticed, objecting to it,' Dimitri said. 'Nor to his
kissing your fingers, even though you made an attempt to
hide the fact. The situation spoke for itself, Miss Gordon!'

'I was taken by surprise!' She glanced from the corner
of her eye at Mitso, gazing adoringly, or so it seemed, into
his fiancée's eyes, and she felt resentment among a whole
host of other reactions. 'You know very well how easily
these situations arise with your brother, Mr Karamalis.
What could I do?'

'Resist,' Dimitri suggested firmly. 'Or perhaps you are
not very adept at resisting good-looking young men,
thespinís; if that is so then you must learn!'

Carey was angrier than she ever remembered being and
from her flushed face, bright angry grey eyes glared at
him across the table as she prepared to make a stand
against his autocratic bullying. 'You have no cause and
no—no *right* to speak to me like that!' she told him crossly.
'I'm here because you insisted I remain; if you don't ap-
prove of me, Mr Karamalis, you'd do better to let me go
home as I planned!'

She glanced uneasily at Niki after she had said it, for
upsetting him at that point was the last thing she wanted,
but Niki wasn't concerned with anything but his breakfast
at the moment. Swiftly returning her attention to the
vaguely menacing figure opposite, she looked at him in a
way that challenged him to do as she said.

'It does not suit me, *thespinís*, and that is an end of it!'

They both continued with breakfast in angry silence,
and when Mitso looked around at her again he raised a
brow, glancing across at his brother. He looked as if he

would have said something, but before he could speak
Despina's soft plump hand touched his cheek and turned
his face in her direction again, smiling and giving Carey a
narrow look of warning from her dark eyes.

It had been instinctive to smile when he looked at her,
and when she realised Dimitri had seen, she started to say
something that he cut across abruptly. Pointing to Niki
and frowning, 'Is it customary to bring the boy to the
table wearing a stained shirt?' he demanded, and Carey
stared at him for a moment before she turned and looked
at Niki.

She had left him to his own devices instead of supervis-
ing him this morning, and some of the fruit preserve he
had put on his buttered roll had found its way down the
front of his light shirt in messy purple streaks. It looked
awful, and she clicked her tongue in annoyance, making
much more of the incident than she would normally have
done, simply because Dimitri was watching her, 'Oh, Niki,
just look at your shirt!'

In normal circumstances he would have grinned at her
sheepishly, then apologised for the mess, but these circumstances were rather different. He had Dimitri's stern black
eyes on him, and both Mitso and Despina were looking on
and smiling, so that he squirmed with embarrassment,
and his lip trembled as he looked up at Carey with eyes
that shimmered with the threat of tears.

'I didn't know it happened,' he told her. 'Honestly,
Carey, I didn't.'

It wasn't his fault, Carey recognised it while he pleaded
with her. She had been too involved with Mitso to supervise him as she usually did, and the blame was hers, so
that she smiled at him as she bent to wipe some of the
mess with her handkerchief. 'Don't worry about it, darling,
you didn't do it on purpose, I just didn't notice what you
were doing.'

'You were perhaps too busy in another direction,'
Dimitri observed, and she looked across at him quickly,

that deep quiet voice slipping like an icy caress along her spine. 'Please see that he puts on a clean shirt before he sees his grandmother, Miss Gordon. She is most particular about cleanliness even in small children.'

Flushed and furious, Carey was already on her feet and clasping Niki's hand tightly, glaring across at Dimitri with eyes that condemned him as thoroughly as he condemned her. 'I don't think you can know very much about small boys, Mr Karamalis,' she told him, 'or you'd know that they have a habit of getting dirty, *very* dirty on occasion, and if Madame Karamalis has brought up three sons I can't believe that the sight of a grubby shirt is going to disturb her unduly!'

She didn't wait to hear what else he had to say, but turned blindly and almost fell on the uneven stone paving in her haste, then went hurrying around the edge of the pool with her head high and hanging on tightly to Niki's hand, heedless of the fact that he was having to practically run to keep pace with her. But no one said anything, that she heard, and she guessed that it wasn't often Dimitri was spoken to as she had just spoken to him; they were probably all too dumbfounded to speak.

Niki skipped and pattered along with her, glancing up at the unfamiliar look of anger on her face and probably seeing it as one more thing to puzzle over, for there had been so many lately. Then it was as if she suddenly remembered he was there, and she looked down at him as they began to climb the stairs, and quite impulsively hugged him.

'Don't worry about your shirt,' she told him. 'I know you didn't do it deliberately, and I *should* have kept an eye on you.'

'He's cross.'

He sounded as if he thought it inevitable that Dimitri was angry, and Carey gave him a rueful smile as she stroked his hair back from his eyes. 'Yes, I'm afraid your uncle *is* cross, but with me, not you.'

'He doesn't like us much, does he?'

Carey was convinced she knew Dimitri's feelings where she was concerned, but she hoped it wasn't true about Niki. 'I think he's just a naturally stern man, darling,' she told him. 'It doesn't necessarily mean he doesn't like people, and he likes you because he's your uncle.'

'Hmm.'

He didn't look entirely convinced, but with the resilience of childhood he had completely recovered his natural exuberance by the time he was dressed in a clean shirt and presented himself for Carey's inspection. She sat in the window, looking out at the countryside, and she had to admit to finding a special kind of magic in the acres of pale-leaved vines and tortured olive trees spread over the hillsides in the hot sun.

It would be good to be free of the villa for a short time, however beautiful it was, and impulsively she put the idea to Niki. 'How would you like to go exploring, Niki? Not too far, just for a walk to look at the countryside; would you like that?'

They had often gone for walks in the London parks and Niki had enjoyed it, because it gave him an opportunity to expend some of his energy, and the prospect of entirely new country delighted him. He was nodding and smiling and his dark eyes gleamed with enthusiasm. 'We could go and find the sea,' he declared excitedly, grasping her hands and pulling her up from the windowsill. 'You said it wasn't very far on the map!'

'Not too far,' Carey agreed cautiously, 'but too far to walk, I think, darling. We'll go a little way today and go and find the sea another day. O.K.?'

'O.K!' He was skipping in his excitement and Carey already felt a little more lighthearted as she followed him. 'Come on, Carey!'

In fact it was almost too hot for walking, certainly it was too hot to walk very far, and Carey soon began to wish she had a hat she could put on. Niki on the other hand seemed completely unaffected, and she supposed he had some kind of inborn tolerance for the heat that came from his mother, for Aliki had never minded how hot it got.

So far they had passed only vineyards, and grapevines grew too low to offer any kind of shade, so that Carey heaved a sigh of relief when they at last reached an olive grove. Rows of grey-twisted trunks and tortuous branches made patches of blessed cool that she found irresistible, despite Niki's frown. 'Just a few minutes,' she pleaded as she dropped down under one of the trees. 'I'm very hot, Niki, and I'd like to sit here for a few minutes and cool off.'

'You all right?' His big eyes clouded with concern for a moment, and she smiled as she reached up and touched his cheek.

'I'm fine, darling, just hot, that's all. When I've had a little rest in the shade we'll perhaps go on a bit farther, although we've come quite a long way already.' Niki looked good for another mile or two, and Carey envied him as she leaned back against the trunk of her tree. 'Why don't you sit down for a few minutes as well, hmm? It's rather nice in the shade.'

Obviously the inactivity didn't appeal at all, and he shook his head. 'I'll just play around here,' he told her. 'There are lots of trees.'

'Well, don't climb them, and stay close, O.K.?' He nodded, and she smiled, settling back against the tree and automatically closing her eyes. 'That's a good boy.'

The ground wasn't nearly as hard as she expected, and she found it was possible to get quite comfortable with her legs curled round under her and leaning against the tree. She listened to Niki playing one of his imaginative games, using a variety of different voices as he acted out some fantasy or other, and the last thing she had in mind was falling asleep.

When she opened her eyes again it was with the awful

realisation that she had done just that, and she sat up quickly, shaking the lethargy from her limbs and the sleep from her brain. It was so incredibly quiet that her heart began a hard, painful beat, for she could neither see nor hear Niki. Scrambling hastily to her feet, she looked around her, one hand brushing over her hair and the other down her dress, and feeling sick with panic suddenly.

'Niki, Niki! Niki, where are you? Niki!'

There was no sound at all but the distant hum of an engine of some kind and the chittering voice of a sparrow in the trees, nothing at all that sounded like a child's voice involved in make-believe. Carey's face drained of colour as nausea clawed at her stomach, for she couldn't believe he'd go very far, not in a strange place.

'Niki-i-i!'

The olive grove bordered the road and she could see across the other side of it to the same sprawling acres of vines and olives, with only a tiny white house right over in the distance, and she felt suddenly and terrifyingly lonely and afraid of this strange country. Sick with panic, she turned automatically back among the crowded olive trees, calling all the time, yet scarcely able to recognise her own voice because it sounded so thin.

'Niki!'

She turned swiftly when she heard a car pull up at the roadside, and she was so desperate to get help that she didn't hesitate to call on a stranger, whoever it might be. Stumbling on the rutted ground and with perspiration beading her upper lip and the lids of her wildly anxious eyes, she went hurrying forward, only to stop dead and stare in horror when the driver of the big Mercedes stepped out on to the road.

She had last seen Dimitri sitting at the breakfast table, having just reproved her for neglecting Niki by failing to supervise his eating; how much more disapproving was he going to be when he discovered that she had allowed him to wander off alone? Her legs were shaking as she approached him, and it was inevitable that he was frowning, so that she brushed a hand across her moist forehead as she stopped in front of him.

'Miss Gordon? What on earth has happened to you? Are you ill?'

'No, no——'

'Where is Nikolas?'

So many questions, and they spun around in her head as she tried to summon her self-control and speak normally. 'I—I don't know where he is, Mr Karamalis.' Her voice shivered and broke, and she could do nothing about the tears in her eyes, although they brought no sign of sympathy from the man facing her, only a deeper frown.

'Are you telling me that you have lost the boy?'

That was exactly what she had done, Carey realised, and Dimitri's black eyes condemned her out of hand for it. There was no hint of compassion in the almost primitive features as he looked down at her, and she knew that however much she appealed for understanding, he wouldn't listen. 'He—he must have wandered off,' she said, and tears muffled her voice as she put a hand to her aching head.

'While you were doing what, Miss Gordon?'

'I still can't believe it,' she told him, 'but I must have fallen asleep. I can't think why, I've never done such a thing before in broad daylight.'

One hand still rested on her forehead and Dimitri frowned. Brushing aside her hand, he placed his own broad palm against her aching head, and his frown deepened. 'You are not accustomed to so much sun,' he observed. 'Does your head ache?'

'A—a bit, now you mention it. I hadn't realised, but it does; I suppose it must be the sun.'

'You will remain here, *out* of the sun, while I attempt to find Nikolas,' he decided with his customary brusqueness.

'He cannot have gone very far.'

'It couldn't have been more than a few minutes,' Carey confirmed. 'But I must insist on helping to find him, Mr Karamalis, it is my fault after all.'

'You will remain here in the shade until I bring him back,' Dimitri argued. 'Let me have no more trouble with you, Miss Gordon, I have sufficient to occupy me, searching for Nikolas. You will sit in the car and remain there until I return, do you understand me?'

'But——'

'*Epiph!*' he swore harshly, 'will you do as I tell you!' He took her arm, gripping her cruelly hard and pulling her towards the car at the edge of the road. He had the door already open when he stopped suddenly and stared at a small group in the distance and making towards them very slowly. The words he used, softly and half under his breath, sounded too much like a prayer to be anything else, and Carey followed the direction of his gaze.

She recognised a mule and a man walking beside it, but it was a second or two before the full significance of a small, black-haired boy riding on the mule's back dawned on her. 'Niki!'

Heaven knew how he had gone so far in such a short time, but relief seemed suddenly to overwhelm her, and her legs trembled so much that they threatened to give way under her. Immediately Dimitri's arm was slipped around her waist and she turned quite instinctively towards him, hiding her face in his shoulder for a moment in sheer relief. What the words meant that he murmured so vehemently, she had no idea, but the vigour and strength of the supporting body was incredibly affecting, even in those circumstances.

'He's all right,' she whispered, turning to look at the little group on the road again, and Dimitri reached down to pull the door wide and he again spoke in that harsh impatient voice.

'Not for much longer!' he threatened darkly, and Carey

gripped his arm as he tried to sit her in the car, fighting his attempt to make her sit down behind the steering wheel.

'Please,' she begged, 'let me go and fetch him, or let the man bring him, he's coming this way.'

She was frantic to get to Niki before he did, but Dimitri was in no mood to be put off his chosen path, and he looked down into her flushed face with his mouth tight and his eyes glowing like jet. 'You are not fit to walk even one step in your present state,' he ordered, and Carey wondered if he had any idea that the light touch he used to brush the hair back from her brow had as much to do with her trembling as the heat and worry about Niki combined. She was held in the tight curve of his arm and the touch of that stunningly virile body played havoc with her senses. 'You will sit in the car until I come back,' he repeated, 'and do not come after me, or I shall be forced to carry you bodily back here and lock you in!'

'Then don't be too hard on him,' she pleaded.

His long fingers curved into the hollow below her breast, and there was a disturbingly earthy, masculine scent about him that made her head spin as much as the heat did. He looked down into her eyes for a moment, then eased her into the driving seat, leaving a warm imprint on her responsive flesh when he took away his hand.

He spared a glance over his shoulder at the approaching mule and its attendants, then leaned down until his face was close to hers. 'He is six years old,' he reminded her, 'and old enough to know the meaning of obedience. Mouska, the man who is bringing him back, should not be coming this way at all, which means that he is neglecting his work to bring him. No doubt Nikolas is enjoying his ride, but he must be made to understand that by wandering off as he did he has caused a great deal of concern and inconvenience.'

'He's a baby!'

'He is a boy,' Dimitri insisted firmly, 'and knows right

from wrong. If he does not, Miss Gordon, you have been remiss in his upbringing!'

'Then punish me, not Niki!'

'*Kólasiz!*' Dimitri swore. 'You are as much a child as Nikolas, and likely to be as much trouble to me, it seems! I consider you have been punished sufficiently by your concern for him; Nikolas's punishment you may safely leave to me, but be sure it will fit the crime!'

He was already striding away from her and Carey felt horribly helpless sitting behind the steering wheel and watching him through the windscreen. She had no right to interfere, she told herself, for Dimitri Karamalis was responsible for Niki from now on, but she wished he had not made that last enigmatic statement sound so grim.

The mule and its companions were closer now and she could make out the expressions on the face of the man as he brought the animal to a halt and lifted Niki down. He seemed to be making some explanation, but from the way he was pointing, it seemed Niki must have gone much farther than she could have guessed, and she once more blamed herself, whatever Dimitri said.

Standing on the road, Niki looked such a tiny figure with his uncle towering over him, and it was clear he was being lectured from the way he hung his head. The man with the mule had turned and was going back the way he came, leaving the two of them there alone, and just briefly Niki's head turned in her direction.

The lecture over, it looked as if Niki would have dashed off towards the car, but he was sternly brought back and made to walk sedately beside his uncle, his small hand clasped firmly in Dimitri's much larger one. Not once did he kick up the dust with the toes of his shoes as he had done when he was walking with her, and he looked so subdued that she ignored Dimitri's instruction and got out of the car, though she simply stood there and waited instead of going to meet them.

She tried to catch Niki's eye, but when she smiled reassuringly at him he only gave her a very faint one in response, so that she felt an immediate surge of anger against the man who held him so firmly. Yet it was curious, although he looked so small and appealing there was such a similarity to the man who walked beside him that there was no mistaking a relationship. Niki was undeniably a Karamalis, and it was becoming increasingly obvious which of them he resembled most.

They came to a halt in front of her and Dimitri let go his hand. 'What do you have to say?' he prompted, and the way Niki glanced up at him before he spoke startled her, for the look was both appealing and trusting.

'I'm sorry I went off, Carey,' he said gravely, 'but I didn't know how con-concerned you'd be. Are you feeling better now?'

'Oh yes, darling, thank you!' She was close to tears and there was a painful choking sensation in her throat that threatened her voice. 'But you frightened me going off like that; it was very, very naughty and I'm cross.'

'Thios Dimitri said you was feeling—faint with concern and I should be 'shamed of myself.'

It was so obviously a quote that Carey wondered how much else he had been told and whether it had been stern enough to have any lasting effect. Even she had to admit that Niki could on occasion be impulsively naughty, but she had never found scolding him very much use, for he could coax her out of her anger all too easily. Something she doubted he could do with Dimitri Karamalis.

'I went a long way,' he began, coming up and standing directly in front of her, and Carey recognised the first attempt to smooth over her anger. 'I got right along there, and then this man with——'

'Nikolas!'

He subsided at once, eyes downcast, but glancing up briefly at the black frown of his formidable uncle. There was mischief in the brief look he gave Carey, but he did not attempt to disobey, and when Dimitri took his hand again he did so quite gently, she noticed, bringing his great height down until he was almost level.

'Remember what I have told you?' he asked, and Niki nodded. 'So!' Dimitri said, and straightened up again, giving his attention to Carey. 'In the circumstances I shall drive you back to the villa before going on; you will be better keeping out of the sun for a while, Miss Gordon, and it is quite a long way to walk back.'

The offer was unexpected, like the concern that prompted it, but Carey had no desire at all to be any further trouble to him. 'Oh, but there's really no need for you to turn back, Mr Karamalis,' she protested. 'I've rested and I can walk back, honestly.'

It was a vain protest, of course, and that firm hand was once more on her arm, guiding her around to the other side of the car, with Niki following and obviously much more interested in the idea of a car ride than she was. 'That is nonsense, and I think you are aware it is,' Dimitri told her. 'You have already been too long in the sun and I do not want to have the inconvenience of having you ill with heat-stroke. When we get back, you will go to your room and rest in the cool.'

'Niki——' she started to protest, and was silenced at once by a raised hand.

'Nikolas may sit with his grandmother and endeavour to learn some more Greek.' He turned to the boy and said something to him in Greek which he did not find very much to his liking, judging by his expression, though he nodded agreement.

'*Né*, Thíos Dimitri.'

His very basic Greek seemed to please his uncle, as much because he had understood the question as for any other reason, Carey thought, and Dimitri placed a hand on his head for a moment and half-smiled. '*Kali*—that is good. You improve every day and very soon now I think we shall have you speaking Greek like a true Karamalis, eh?'

It was staggering to see how readily Niki lapped up his approval, and for some curious reason Carey suddenly felt a sense of loss, as if she had been cut off from Niki's exclusive affection. 'What about Carey?' he asked his uncle, and his apparent lack of fear was another thing that surprised her.

Dimitri paused with his hand on the door handle and his deep black eyes were fixed on her with an intensity that set her pulse racing wildly and brought an added flush of colour to her cheeks as she hastily avoided them. 'She may also learn Greek if she wishes to,' he said, and the tone of his voice stroked along her back like a caress.

'No, thank you!' She spoke up quickly and sounded alarmingly breathless. 'I have no gift for languages, and Aliki failed miserably trying to teach me to speak Greek. Also there isn't a lot of point, is there, as I'm not staying all that long?'

His mouth showed a hint of mockery, as did his eyes, and the hand that still held her arm squeezed very slightly into her flesh. 'But have we not settled that matter?' he asked.

'*You've* settled it,' Carey retorted, unable to resist it. 'I was prepared to leave for home after a few days, Mr Karamalis.'

'Home.' He echoed the word softly as he opened the car door, and he determinedly held her reluctant gaze as he was pressed briefly against her. 'Do you not have a saying in England, Miss Gordon—home is where the heart is? You may find in time that you have no desire to leave Greece.'

Without quite knowing why, Carey suspected he might one day be right, but she had no intention of admitting it yet, and certainly not at that moment. 'I think that's unlikely,' she told him as he held open the car door for her with one hand while the other tried to put her into the front seat. It was an attempt she resisted, turning instead to draw Niki forward and put him in the seat beside the driver. 'You'd like to ride in the front, wouldn't you, Niki? Come on, jump in!'

Whether or not he would have done as she said, she was never given the opportunity to find out, for he was firmly put aside and she was herself practically forced to sit down. 'You will ride in the back, Nikolas,' Dimitri told him, and closed the door on her.

He put Niki into the back, then went striding round and got in beside her. His swift, catlike movements gave her a strange curling sensation in her stomach, and there was an aura about him that stirred every nerve in her body. Turning in his seat, he fixed his black eyes on her steadily, and Carey wondered what she was to be charged with now.

'You are unaccustomed to riding in cars, Miss Gordon?' he asked, and she gave him a brief, suspicious look from the corner of her eye before she answered.

'I haven't very often ridden in one,' she admitted. 'Whenever Niki and I went anywhere we usually took a taxi, or sometimes went on the bus.'

'I thought so.' He started up the car and she frowned at him because she was curious and he looked like leaving her so. Then he half turned his head again. 'It is a dangerous practice to put a child into the front seat of a car,' he told her. 'He is much safer in the back.'

'Oh, I see, I didn't realise that.'

'Obviously.' He put the car in gear and as they set off along the deserted road he once again turned those disturbing black eyes on her. 'In my country women do not argue, Miss Gordon,' he said coolly, and Carey caught her breath at the sheer arrogance of him.

'Mr Karamalis, if you think——'

'I suggest you lean back your head and relax,' Dimitri advised, as if she had not spoken. 'You have had a little too much sun and too much emotional upset this morning and you should take matters easily for an hour or two, eh?'

'Are you suggesting that I'm—overwrought because I object to the way you speak to me?' she demanded, and could scarcely believe the slight curve that showed for a moment at the corners of his mouth.

'I am suggesting that you learn to adapt to your new environment, Miss Gordon, you will find it so much more easy for you if you do. And you *have* had a little too much sun, also you *are* overwrought, so why not do as I say and lean back your head?'

Incredibly she found herself doing as he said, for there was an almost hypnotic quality about that deep, quiet voice, and argument had already proved futile with this man. So she sighed and leaned back in her seat, resigned for the moment, but by no means subdued.

CHAPTER FOUR

IT was a little over three weeks since she and Niki arrived in Greece, and just lately Carey had found herself having to rethink quite a few hastily formed opinions. Not least of them was Niki's relationship with Dimitri, for there seemed to be a definite rapport between them that was, to her at least, quite unexpected. It pleased her for Niki's sake that he seemed to have taken to the sternest of his three uncles, but on the other hand it left her feeling that she had been ousted from her place as the most important person in his life.

When they lived in England his natural father had taken very little interest in him, seeing him merely as an unfortunate consequence of his affair with Aliki, so that the firm hand of masculine authority was a new experience for him. But one that he was not altogether averse to, judging by his attitude towards Dimitri ever since the day he had lectured him for wandering off on his own. Seeing how subdued he had been on that occasion, Carey had expected resentment, but instead he seemed to appreciate having a man in charge, and it occurred to her that on the subject of Dimitri, she and Niki no longer saw eye to eye.

Niki liked his grandmother too, which was more understandable, and he had gone off with her quite happily that morning to visit relatives in Athens. Rather at a loss without him, Carey found herself a book and made her way towards the pool, but she hadn't gone more than a few steps from the house when Mitso caught up with her, and guessing what was in his mind, she almost turned back; she was always very wary where Mitso was concerned.

It being Saturday he wasn't required to go to the office in Athens, so he was looking for something to amuse him, and seeing Carey he obviously decided that she was exactly what he was looking for. He approached her smiling broadly and so sure of his welcome that Carey wondered whether there was ever anyone more sure of himself than Mitso. Yet despite her being on her guard with him her senses still responded, and she believed he was well aware of it; that he banked on it even.

'What are you doing this morning while Mamá has taken Nikolas to see Thía Helene?' he asked as he walked along with her, and his hand reached for hers, squeezing it lightly. 'You have some free time, eh?'

Carey showed him the book she had in her hand. 'I'm going to sit by the pool and read,' she told him. 'I don't often have the opportunity.'

'And I seldom have the opportunity to see you alone,' Mitso complained in his strongly pedantic English. 'You always have that wretched child with you.'

She never liked his attitude towards Niki, and usually let him see how she felt. 'If you're talking about Niki,' she said, 'your brother pays me to be always with him, and I enjoy looking after him, Mitso.'

'But not every minute of every day,' Mitso insisted, and

squeezed her hand again. 'This morning while Mamá has charge of him you can relax a little. You can spare some time for me, eh?'

The trouble with Mitso was that he was alarmingly persuasive when he put his mind to it, but she had made up her mind what she ought to do, and she determinedly freed her hand. 'I was rather looking forward to my book, Mitso.'

His dark eyes seeking to persuade her, Mitso leaned his head down and looked into her face. 'Oh, but surely you would prefer to do something more exciting with your free time. Surely there is somewhere that you have wished to go to; somewhere you would have visited if you had not been obliged to take Nikolas with you?'

It was true, though Carey hesitated to tell him so, for it was evident what he was leading up to, and agreeing to go anywhere with him could set a dangerous precedent, she thought. 'I'll be quite happy with my book,' she insisted, but she felt very unsure how strong her will would prove to be if Mitso put himself out to persuade her.

'You do not like Greece?'

How could she answer that? The Greeks were very proud of their country and did not take kindly to those who belittled it. 'What I've seen of it I've liked very much,' she told him cautiously, and Mitso laughed.

'And how much is that? I drove you here from the airport, and you once took a walk with Nikolas, when Dimitri drove you back in his car. You have been nowhere else, have you?'

'No.'

She made the admission unwillingly because she knew she would demolish her own argument if she said any more. Often she felt she would like to see some of the ancient beauties of Greece, but allowing Mitso to take her wouldn't be wise at all. With Despina Glezos hovering jealously in the background, and the Karamalis family viewing his bold flirtations with a disapproving eye, Mitso was the last person she should choose to show her the sights.

'Then you must see more of our country,' he decided. 'You would like to, eh?'

Faced with an outright question, how could she deny it, whatever the dangers? 'Of course I'd love to see the temples and palaces and the wonderful churches, but I'll go sightseeing after I leave here, when I'm on my way home. There's time yet.'

'Of course there is,' Mitso agreed readily. 'But it is not good that you go nowhere now. There is somewhere special you would like to see, eh? The Acropolis perhaps, or the Sanctuary of Artemis at Brauron? I will take you wherever you wish to go!'

Carey folded her hands tightly together over the book she held, partly because it kept them out of his reach, but also because it helped to strengthen her resistance. 'It's very kind of you,' she began, 'but I don't think——'

'*Ehé!*' Mitso exclaimed impatiently. 'I cannot believe that you are so concerned with what Despina will say because I drive you to see some of the sights! I am anxious only that you should see something of my country, Carey, and there must be something that you have a special longing to see. You have only to tell me and I will drive you there!'

When she felt herself wavering, she clasped her hands more tightly than ever to stiffen her resistance, but Mitso noticed and frowned. Taking the book from her, he threw it down on the garden and grasped both her hands in his, looking down into her face and bringing the added persuasion of his dark eyes to bear. The brief upward glance she gave him was her undoing, and she shook her head even while she described the place she had so often thought of visiting.

'There's a little temple of some kind, not very far away. I can see it from my bedroom window, among the trees on the hillside, and it always looks so—I don't know exactly,

I can't describe how it makes me feel. It's quite small and very pretty.'

Mitso's eyes had the gleam of satisfaction as he raised her hands to his lips and he kissed her fingers lightly, laughing softly. 'You choose well, *oréos mou*, and of course I will drive you there. You should know that also this involves a long walk uphill, yes?'

'It won't take long?' She was still anxious about going with him, and also she was thinking about Madame Karamalis coming back with Niki and learning that she had gone sightseeing with Mitso in her absence.

'It will not take long to get there,' Mitso agreed, and kissed her hands again. Looking directly into her eyes, he smiled. 'But you are not forbidden to leave the house, Carey, no one has told you so, I am sure. Not even Dimitri would dare to issue such an order!'

'Oh no, of course he hasn't!' She made a face, mocking her own feeling where Dimitri was concerned. 'I could go out, I know, it's just that so far I haven't made the effort.'

'Then today you will, eh?'

Much as she rued her own weakness, Carey saw herself with little option now, and she nodded. It was all he needed, and Mitso took her hand, changing direction and leading her along the path that took them to the yard where the cars were garaged, smiling now that he had got his way. It was a surprise to both of them to find someone there ahead of them, and Carey caught her breath when Dimitri raised his head from under the bonnet of the Mercedes he usually drove.

Seeing him messing about with the engine was unexpected too, for she had never seen him as a physical man to that extent, and he looked very much the mechanic as he straightened up, wiping his hands on a rag while he fixed his eyes on her. The steady, unwavering gaze had its customary effect, and she could never remain unmoved by Dimitri, though sometimes she despaired of her own susceptibility, and at times even resented it.

He was very little taller than Mitso and yet he seemed so much more overpowering, and that aura of sensuality about him stunned her senses, making her aware of every little detail about him. A light blue shirt showed off his dark complexion, and she sometimes wondered if he was more self-aware than he appeared, and chose the clothes he wore with the deliberate intention of making the most of his considerable sex-appeal.

The shirt was thin, and when he reached up to close the bonnet of the car the darkness of his body showed through it, the open neck revealing a long vee of brown throat. A pair of old and crumpled fawn slacks still fitted close about his lean waist and hips and stretched over muscular legs as he came striding across the yard to them. And Carey was appalled by the sudden weakness of her own legs.

Mitso had evidently decided that the situation called for bravado, and he spoke up before Dimitri reached them, telling him exactly what he proposed to do and quite blatantly defying him to do anything about it. 'I am driving Carey into the country,' he told him. 'She wishes to see the temple of Artemis at Naós Lófos and I have promised to take her.'

Dimitri so obviously disapproved that Carey hastened to make her own position clear too, although she had so far said nothing against the trip. 'I've been wanting to see it for some time,' she told him. 'I can see it from my bedroom window and it looks so pretty up there among the trees. I think I'm entitled to some time off, aren't I, Mr Karamalis? I haven't had any since I came.'

It was a direct challenge to him to deny her the trip and Dimitri recognised it as such. His black eyes watched her with that same disturbing steadiness still, and made her realise how aggressive she must have sounded, before he'd even said a word against her going. 'I have no objection at all to you having time off, Miss Gordon,' he confirmed, in a voice that was guaranteed to put her firmly in her place, 'nor do I blame you for wishing to see the sanctuary of Artemis, it is very beautiful.'

'Thank you.'

The colour was warm in her cheeks because he had managed to make her feel as she did without even raising his voice. 'I should point out, however,' he went on, 'that my brother is expected at the home of his fiancée; it is a regular thing that has gone on ever since they became betrothed. Also the road to Naós Lófos leads past the Villa Glezos and I feel it would be rather—indiscreet in the circumstances for Mitso to be seen driving past with you.'

How neatly he managed to work things around to his way, Carey thought furiously, and knew she hadn't a leg to stand on if she was not to appear as uncaring as Mitso often did about Despina Glezos's feelings. 'I have to agree,' she said in a small voice that made her disappointment obvious. And she was disappointed, no matter how much persuasion it had taken to get her to agree to the trip.

Mitso looked defiantly sulky, thrusting his hands into the pockets of his slacks and hunching his shoulders. 'It would not have mattered to miss one day,' he complained in the face of his brother's calm acceptance of the situation. 'It was not easy to persuade Carey to come with me, and now that she is anxious to go you ask me to disappoint her.'

'Oh, but it really doesn't matter that much,' Carey insisted. 'I can go any time and see the temple, it isn't very far away after all. I could even take a taxi so far and then walk up the hill, if it comes to that.'

Dimitri was still using the rag to wipe oil from his hands and he did not look at her while he spoke. 'That won't be necessary,' he said, 'and you need not be disappointed, Miss Gordon. If you will give me time to clean up and change, I am free for the next few hours and I will be quite willing to drive you there.'

Carey looked up swiftly, for the softness of persuasion in his voice was unmistakable and brought an urgent flutter to her heartbeat. Mitso, in contrast, spoke with the harsh-

ness of anger, and his eyes blazed as he saw himself being
out-manoeuvred. It could not be very often it happened,
Carey guessed, and he resented it bitterly.

'*Epiph!*' he swore. 'Why should Carey wish to go with
you?'

His head slightly back, Dimitri looked at him from
below heavy lids, his black eyes challenging. 'You think
she will be disappointed?' he suggested, and a faint curve
on his wide mouth suggested it was very unlikely. 'You
will admit, Mitso, that I am better informed on such matters as the ancient temples than you are, hmm?'

'History!' Mitso jeered, and Dimitri immediately took
him up on it, his eyes gleaming.

'Is that not the customary reason for visiting ancient
temples?' he asked coolly, and Mitso swore quietly but
virulently in his own tongue.

To Carey it was incredible that they should be arguing
over which of them should take her, and she listened to
them in growing wonder. It was true she would have
enjoyed going with Mitso, but she had no doubt that
looking at the ruined temple would not have been the
main attraction as far as he was concerned. But the
thought of going with Dimitri brought a different kind of
anticipation altogether, and one that set her whole body
throbbing with expectation.

His eyes were turned on her again, heavy-lidded and
frankly persuasive. 'Do you still wish to go, Miss Gordon?'
he asked, and she nodded unhesitatingly.

'If you have the time,' she said, and Dimitri nodded
gravely.

'I will not be very long.'

Mitso, out-manoeuvred and furious about it, turned
from them and went striding off back the way they had
come, with his hands still in his pockets and his shoulders
hunched. Carey as she watched him go felt just a twinge
of conscience about him, and heaven knew what was going
on behind Dimitri's dark, enigmatic gaze as he followed

his brother's thrusting progress through the shrubbery.

'Will you wait here for me or come back to the house?'

His voice brought her back to earth, and Carey felt the colour once more flood into her face as she looked up at him briefly. 'I—I think I'll wait here,' she said. 'And please don't hurry on my account.'

He smiled faintly as he turned and hurled the rag he had been using in through the garage door. 'Of course I *will*,' he said, and Carey took note of the unmistakable satisfaction in his manner.

He must be accustomed to victory, but to Carey there was something very satisfying about the fact that he seemed so pleased about this particular victory.

Carey had so often seen the temple from her window and found something quite beautiful in its slender columns glimpsed at on a wooded hillside. To have caught only glimpses of it teased the senses, and she could not wait to see it close to and in its entirety.

But the drive there made her realise how much farther away it was than it looked from her window, and the end of the drive was by no means the end of the trip. As Mitso had warned her, there was still a long climb up the wooded hillside, but that proved to be much more pleasurable than she expected, for the trees did a lot to keep the heat of the sun at bay, and the ground smelled richly of dead leaves and the cool aroma of earth.

There was a clearing above them and for the last few yards Dimitri lent her a hand, his strong fingers curving into her flesh and adding to the wild, erratic beating of her heart. Even under the trees it was warm and she was glad of the thin blue cotton dress she was wearing, for it had no sleeves and the scooped neck allowed the ever-present wind to her skin.

'We are almost there.'

She turned her head when he spoke and contented herself with a nod because she was so breathless, and she noticed that he had opened the neck of his shirt still further, until the edges fluttered in the wind, cooling not only his chest but a glimpse of hard, flat stomach as well. There was something infinitely exciting about climbing a wooded hillside with someone as earthily masculine as Dimitri, and the flush on her cheeks wasn't entirely due to the heat.

'Be careful, there are some fallen pillars in the grass.'

They had arrived at a small grass-grown plateau at the summit of the hill, and she stood for a second breathing hard and looking at the temple for the first time without an obscuring screen of trees about it. It was less perfectly preserved than it appeared from a distance, but it was still beautiful, and Carey thrilled to its honey-coloured columns and tiled floor, despite the fact that most of the tiles were broken and barely recognisable.

'It's beautiful,' she whispered as they walked into the fragile-looking shell of the temple, and only when she looked directly at him did she realise that Dimitri was looking at her rather than at their surroundings.

The climb had made them both slightly breathless and his voice had a curious huskiness when he answered her that she found even more affecting than usual. 'It is as beautiful as the goddess whose temple it is,' he said, 'and I never tire of it.'

Turning her head, she looked into his eyes for a moment, and something in the atmosphere of the place was as heady as wine, playing havoc with her senses so that she clung desperately to normality while she could. 'Of course you know all about the gods and goddesses, don't you?' she asked. 'At least that was the impression I got when you told Mitso you knew more about these things than he did.'

She gazed around her as she spoke, feeling that steady black gaze on her still, and it was a second or two before Dimitri replied. 'I know more than Mitso does,' he agreed, 'but Mitso knows very little.'

She strolled off a little way, still dangerously lightheaded with the wonderful atmosphere of the place, laughing and not really thinking of what she was saying. 'Poor Mitso!'

The brief silence was telling. 'Would you rather Mitso had brought you?'

Carey turned, and her heart was racing wildly as she looked at him, still trying hard to keep things on a practical level. 'No, of course not. After all, I came to see the temple, and you know more about them than Mitso does.'

It was difficult to know what was going on behind those black eyes, but they watched her still, and disturbed her more than they had ever done. 'Is this your first look at a Greek temple, or have you seen others?'

'How could I?' She gazed up at the broken roof of the building rather than at him. 'I've never been to Greece until I came with Niki, although I've seen pictures, and often thought how lovely it would be to stand in the sun where someone had stood thousands of years before me. Now I'm relying on you to tell me all about it.'

'Very well.' He moved across to her, standing where the warmth of his body just touched her through the thin stuff of her dress, and his voice still had traces of the unfamiliar huskiness that shivered along her spine like the touch of a light fingertip. 'This is one of the smallest temples to Artemis in existence, but one of the loveliest, I think, and as yet undiscovered by the tourist.'

'Of which you count me one!'

The challenge wasn't a serious one, and she laughed as she glanced at him over her shoulder. 'I did not say so,' Dimitri denied gravely, and took her hand, bringing that urgent, rapid heartbeat into being once again. 'Come, if you wish to see it all, the altar is here.'

Carey followed him obediently over a floor littered with broken marble and shattered tiles, her hand still firmly clasped by strong fingers, and he paused before a quite incredibly well preserved altar stone. Such was the atmosphere of the place that Carey could almost feel the pres-

ence of past worshippers, hear the murmur of their voices
in the wind that blew in through the broken walls from
the hillside.

'Artemis was the goddess of the hunt, wasn't she?' she
asked, and turned to look at him for confirmation.

The look she saw in his eyes brought swift colour to her
cheeks, and as they stood there before the ancient altar
she felt a sudden thrill of exultation. She trembled and
tried hard not to let him know it, but those firm, hard
fingers still held hers and he must feel their trembling.

'She was also the goddess of the moon,' he said. 'Can
you not see her standing here in her special place, cool
and fair and beautiful?'

As he spoke Carey looked at the armless creature with
only half her face remaining, standing in the curved niche
behind the altar, and she could imagine her just as Dimitri
described her. Though with her conception of the Greeks
as typified by the Karamalises, she could visualise their
gods only as dark and sultry.

'You think she would be fair?' she queried.

Without speaking Dimitri reached round and took her
shoulder-length fair hair in his hands, twisting it into a
knot which he rested on the nape of her neck. 'I am sure
of it,' he murmured in a voice that had the softness of a
caress.

Shivering at the lingering lightness of his hands on her
neck, Carey stood unmoving. A glimpse of sky looked
down at them through the broken roof like a benign eye,
and a shaft of sunlight flooding in through the same opening captured them in its heart, as if the gods were smiling
on them. It touched her hair and gilded it with light, and
the shadow of half-lowered lashes darkened her eyes to the
colour of rain clouds; and she trembled because of the way
Dimitri was looking at her.

Nothing seemed quite real, and she was touched by
feelings that she had no control over, a dreamlike sense of
unreality that alarmed her briefly so that she reached up

and pulled at the knot of hair on her neck. As she shook
it free until it cascaded about her shoulders once more, a
small shiver of laughter escaped her.

'I hadn't realised how dangerously affecting these ancient places can be,' she said. 'I don't know whether it's the
wind, or the silence, or just——'

'The magic of the ancient gods?' Dimitri suggested
softly, and it was too close to her own wild speculation to
be comforting. She had never imagined Dimitri as a
romantic, affected by the same kind of magic as she was
herself, but it seemed she was wrong, and realising it was
oddly disturbing.

'I don't know what it is,' she whispered, 'but it's curious
the effect it has, whatever it is.'

Nothing about the watching eyes mocked her impres-
sionability, she noted, but rather they seemed to understand perfectly. 'It has the magic of ages,' he said, 'and
you are a willing devotee.' Reaching for her hand again,
he drew her across the litter of destruction to a broken
archway that seemed to Carey to look out into infinity.
'There is more,' Dimitri promised.

Standing in the archway it was possible to see how the
effect was achieved, for the hillside dropped away sharply
from the plateau on which the temple stood, and gave the
impression that it hung in space. What seemed like miles
below them the familiar acres of vines sprawled endlessly,
and a cluster of little houses spread out in the sun like
squat white mushrooms. From up there on the plateau it
was like looking down from Mount Olympus itself.

'You see below there?' Dimitri's voice asked, close to
her ear, and she followed his pointing finger. 'All the way
down the hill, you see them?'

Carey could just pick them out; a series of what must
once have been huge stone steps cut into the hillside, but
which were now almost completely engulfed in grass and
trees. 'Steps?' He nodded, and she shook her head, feeling
slightly dizzy as she looked down. 'It's—it's like being on

the edge of eternity.'

'Or close to heaven,' he suggested softly.

Dimitri was standing immediately behind her and very slightly to one side, and the nearness of his lean virility had as much to do with the way she was feeling as the exotic setting. She had never been able to remain unmoved by him, whatever the circumstances, and in this strangely affecting place he seemed so much a part of the erotic unreality that her senses responded even more wildly. It was too easy to imagine him a man-god, practised in the art of seduction and knowing that he had only to raise a finger and she would yield.

Common sense would have told her that the outcome was always in her hands, but the magic was too powerful for the moment, and she was responding to it like someone in a dream. The warmth of his breath on her neck raised her pulse to a rapid urgency that she could not hope to control, and the touch of his naked chest against her back seemed to burn her flesh through the thinness of her dress. She was shivering, and she heard what he was saying only faintly, through the clamour of her heart beat.

'Long before Artemis was worshipped here this place belonged to the nymph Iphigenia. She was a symbol of fertility, and the women came to pray to her that they might be fruitful. I think perhaps it is the warm, sensual presence of Iphigenia that we feel in the air here, rather than the cool virginity of Artemis, hmm?'

His voice was low-pitched and faintly husky, and while he spoke his long fingers lightly stroked strands of hair from her neck so that she closed her eyes briefly and clenched her hands in an attempt to control her racing heart. 'She was here before Artemis?' Her laughter was soft and tremulous. 'I didn't know there was anything before the Olympians.'

'There was always Greece!' Dimitri purred softly into her ear, and impulse made her half turn her head and look at him over her shoulder.

A hint of a smile touched her lips, teasing and provocative, although she wasn't fully aware of it. 'And always women wanting sons to please their husbands?'

'Of course!'

'Sons! Does no one ever pray for daughters?'

There was gentle mockery in her smile and her lips were parted, her eyes shimmering with an excitement that touched every nerve in her body, and she caught her breath audibly when he bent his head suddenly and pressed his lips to the side of her neck. 'Other men's daughters,' he murmured. 'How otherwise would we get out sons?'

To Carey it seemed she had run too far and too fast, and she was breathing quickly and erratically as she looked deep into his eyes for a second before turning her face into his shoulder. His hands slid around her until they rested just below her breasts, pressing her back against his hard masculinity, making her aware of every muscle in his body straining her to him.

'Carey!'

She offered no resistance at all when he turned her towards him, and for a moment, when his eyes looked into hers, it was as if he looked right into her heart. He spoke in his own tongue, and there was a ragged huskiness in his voice as he pulled her into his arms, and the faint murmur of sound she made died under the force of his mouth.

It was a fierce, possessive mouth that drew every vestige of breath from her, leaving her soft and yielding to the hands that pressed into her back until her body bowed to the overwhelming dominance of his. When she reached up and wound her bare arms about his neck, it was in response to a wild abandon over which she had no control.

Then he bent his head to her shoulder and the bristly harshness of his hair brushed her cheek, and she closed her eyes as she turned her face and touched its thick blackness with her lips. With his head bowed it seemed he looked curiously vulnerable suddenly, and she cradled his head to her breast in a tender, exultant caress.

Carey never really knew what brought her back to earth so abruptly, unless it was the sudden sharp burst of sound from a group of quarrelling sparrows up in the roof—a shrill, commonplace sound that had no place in her dream world, so that she drew back quickly, struggling against the hands that still sought to hold her, and alarmed by the violence of her own emotions; stunned by the realisation that it had been Dimitri who kissed her like that.

Suddenly and confusingly shy of him, she stepped aside and clasped her hands about one of the marble pillars, standing with her back half to him and wondering dazedly how it had happened. She had never denied to herself that she found him attractive, but it was hard to believe that she had yielded so readily and with such passion, and her heart pounded like a drum.

Was it that brief, provocative moment when she had teased him that made him act as he had? she wondered, and pressed her forehead to the cool marble pillar. Had he seen it as an invitation and presumed she wanted him to react as Mitso would have done?

'Do not tell me you are shocked!' The thick harshness of his voice suggested that passion had not died, but had changed temper, and she turned her head swiftly to stare at him. 'I cannot believe you can be shocked by one kiss,' he declared, and his eyes gleamed like polished jet between their thick lashes. 'Nor will I believe that is the first time you have been kissed!'

There was a hard straight line to his mouth that completely banished the heady excitement of the last few minutes, and Carey felt so shaken by the change that she could only shake her head. She had never in her life before behaved as she had just done with Dimitri, yet he seemed to think it was perfectly normal behaviour for her.

'I'm not shocked, and I have been kissed before,' she said, trying desperately to steady her voice, 'but I'm not in the habit of behaving like that with every man I meet.'

'Was it not what you expected?' Dimitri demanded, and she knew he was referring to his brother.

'Not from you,' she said huskily, and kept her hands tightly around the pillar because she needed its support.

It wasn't the right thing to have said, and she realised it the moment she saw the way his eyes glittered. 'Because you think me less a man than my brother?' he asked, so softly that she knew exactly how tightly he was holding on to his self-control. 'You misjudge me, *thespinís*, because I do not pursue you with the same predatory determination as he does!'

'Because you don't—didn't seem the type!' Carey argued, and tried to explain how easy it had been for her to be lulled into a sense of false judgment. 'You're always so—so formal, so stern. You don't even use my first name as Mitso does, just now was the first time you've ever called me Carey, and I always get the impression that I'm being firmly kept in my place. Not that it bothers me because it's quite common between employer and employee, but when you suddenly step out of character you can't blame me if I'm confused!'

Her eyes were shadowed and unhappy, she couldn't deny it, and they met his only briefly before she turned away again to look at the sunny hillside and the unchanging sky. The magic had receded until there was no fragment of it left, and she could have wept for something she feared she might never find again. This could be the moment when he decided it was time she went back to England, and every nerve in her body clamoured against him being so heartless.

'Have you seen all you wish to see here?'

The question was so quietly put that Carey stared at him for a moment as she tried once again to bring herself back to earth. It was too hard to believe that he was as completely untouched by what had happened as he appeared to be; that he looked upon it as an interlude that was over, and was now ready to leave. But if it was so, then there was no point in delaying.

She said nothing, she didn't even nod, but turned and walked back across the temple, picking her way over the fallen pillars and broken tiles on the sun-spattered floor. Carefully avoiding coming too close to him, she went on without pause, out into the sunshine and on down the hillside without a backward glance at the little temple whose magic had been so briefly potent.

She knew he followed her, for he was bound to, but she kept ahead of him, and she was breathing hard by the time she got back to the car, though she was bound to wait for him to unlock it for her. Standing with her back against the door, she kept her eyes downcast, her gaze on a point somewhere near her feet, until he came to join her.

He stopped immediately in front of her and she gasped when he spanned a hand about her jaw and lifted her head so that she instinctively looked up at him. 'I shall not apologise,' he told her in a flat voice. 'I have never yet been required to apologise for kissing a pretty woman, and I shall not make you the exception!'

As if to add force to his statement, he bent and pressed his mouth to hers, digging his long fingers into her jaw to prevent her from turning her head away. But Carey did not try to turn away, she suffered the fierce bruising pressure of his mouth without flinching while despairing of the way her heart beat so responsively, and the yearning, uncontrollable need of her body for his.

'You think Mitso would have let you escape so easily?' he demanded, and Carey noted that his voice was noticeably softer, though the pressure of his fingers was still hard.

'I—I know he wouldn't,' Carey whispered, and raised her eyes suddenly to look directly into his. 'That's why I didn't want to go with him.'

His hold on her relaxed but remained, and he was shaking his head as he looked down at her mouth in a way that aroused those fluttering responses again. 'Yet you *were* going with him,' he reminded her, and just for a second his mouth crooked into a half-smile. 'You are not good at saying no, eh, *mikros ena*?' Without waiting for confirmation, he unlocked the door and saw her into the car, and as he closed the door he murmured something in his own tongue that she did not understand.

With her hands pressed tightly together Carey made a slight, instinctive move to avoid contact when he got in beside her, but instead of starting the car, he half turned in his seat and sat looking at her for a moment or two. Then he slid a finger under her chin and turned her to face him with a gentleness that was in direct contrast to his recent violence.

Thinking she knew what was coming, Carey put her fear into words. 'I suppose now you're going to send me back to England?'

'You think so?'

She looked at him reproachfully. 'I'd like an answer,' she said, 'so that I know where I stand.'

'You stand where you have always stood, Carey,' he said, and his use of her first name brought an unexpected thrill of pleasure. 'Are you happy with us—with living at the Villa Karamalis?'

'Why—yes, of course, and Niki loves it now he's got used to you all.'

'I am not so concerned with him at the moment,' Dimitri informed her quietly. 'I have seen the way you look sometimes, and I have wondered if you are—how is it?—putting on a face for Nikolas's benefit.'

'I'm not, I promise you, and I can't think what—look it is you mean.'

'No?' His finger supported her chin while his eyes searched her face, watching every expression that flitted across it.

'If I look a bit strained sometimes,' she said, choosing each word carefully, 'it's because I feel—I know that some

of your family resent me, not for my own sake but Niki's.'
Since he did not deny it, she went on, gathering confidence
and speaking out because it was something she felt deeply
about. 'I can understand Damon's feelings to some extent,
he's had his grandmother to himself for the past fifteen
years, but how can grown-up people resent a little boy?
However they felt about his mother, it isn't Niki's fault.'

'There are a number of reasons,' Dimitri told her, and
he too seemed to be choosing his words with care. 'One is
the Karamalis Company. It is run exclusively by the
family, the male members, of course, and at the moment
that means, Andoni, Mitso and myself; when Damon
comes of age he will automatically become a board
member and take his share of the company, that is how
we work. You can see how the advent of Nikolas changes
things, because when he becomes my adopted son he will
not only take his own share when he comes of age, but
also in time, inherit mine.'

Carey stared at him. This was news indeed, and she did
not know quite what to make of it. 'You—you're going to
try and adopt Niki?'

'I shall not only try, I shall succeed,' Dimitri assured
her. 'In the circumstances there is no impediment to my
adopting him as my son.'

Carey looked at him, touched by something in-
expressibly tender suddenly, and her voice was soft. 'You
love him that much?'

It was impossible to penetrate the thick barrier of his
lashes to tell exactly what was in his eyes, and he had
them lowered. 'He is a Karamalis,' he said, 'and he needs
a father.'

Carey felt as if she had been dealt a blow, and she
shook her head as she stared at him in dismay. Her heart
went out to Niki at the mercy of his practical, unfeeling
family, and as always she leapt to his defence. 'Of course,'
she said in a small tight voice that shook slightly. 'He's a
Karamalis and he has to be made respectable! You have

no more affection for him than Mitso has, and he doesn't like children at all!'

'That is something that will change when he has children of his own,' Dimitri said with quiet matter-of-factness, and Carey vaguely noted his lack of reaction to her charge. She had expected him to be angry, but he wasn't, and she didn't understand it.

'And suppose *you* have children of your own?' she asked. 'What happens to Niki then?'

'Why, he takes his place as my eldest son, of course.' He made the observation so coolly that Carey could do no more than shake her head.

'Oh, you're so—so matter-of-fact!' she despaired.

'I am practical,' Dimitri declared. 'As he is placed at the moment Nikolas has no claim at all to a place in Karamalis and Company, and Mitso for one would like to see that situation continue. He is to marry at the end of next month and he is thinking of his own sons, of course.' He turned swiftly and looked directly into her eyes. 'Did he tell you the wedding date?' he asked, and Carey could not imagine why he thought Mitso's plans interested her to that extent.

'I didn't know when it was,' she told him, 'but then there's no reason why I should be told, is there? If you'll forgive me saying so, I can't help feeling sorry for Despina Glezos, or any girl who marries someone like Mitso!'

'He would not be your choice?' he asked, and Carey denied it hotly and adamantly.

'Definitely not!' Dimitri had turned and was starting the engine, and she studied that dark, stern profile for a moment while he was preoccupied. There was surely never a more puzzling and enigmatic man than Dimitri Karamalis, and she wondered just how seriously he thought she took Mitso's determined efforts at seduction. 'I don't take him seriously, you know,' she ventured, and he turned his head again briefly to look at her.

'You should. No Greek likes being rebuffed by a woman,

and you should understand that Mitso will go on trying until he succeeds.'

Briefly she recalled his own anger when he considered he had been rebuffed by her only recently, and she placed her hands tightly together on her lap. 'He *won't* succeed, Mr Karamalis! I'm not in the habit of having casual affairs, and particularly not with an engaged man! You may not believe it, but I have very strong powers of resistance and I do know right from wrong!'

'Oh, but I do believe it,' Dimitri observed quietly, as he set the car in motion. 'I am counting on it!'

CHAPTER FIVE

NIKI obviously still wasn't very sure what being adopted meant, but Carey was doing her best to explain it to him. Although it was several weeks since Dimitri had told her his plan, nothing had been said to Niki until now, and Carey was rather surprised that the job of breaking the news to him had been given to her.

They were beside the pool, just the two of them at the moment, and Carey was hoping for time to get the idea across to him before anyone else joined them, for the pool was a favourite gathering place, especially at weekends. 'What it really means,' she told Niki, 'is that Thíos Dimitri will be your *papá*. O.K.?'

Niki nodded. On occasion he could look quite disconcertingly like the man they were discussing, and this was one of them, for his brows were drawn and his normally soft, childish mouth was set in a firm line as he concentrated. 'You mean he won't be my Thíos Dimitri any more?'

'Well, yes, of course, he'll still be your uncle, Niki, but he'll also be your *papá*. I know it isn't very easy to under-

stand, but what it amounts to is that Thíos Dimitri loves
you enough to want to make you his little boy.' She took
his hand and held it while she smiled at him encouragingly. 'Very soon now you'll be going with him to see a
rather important man in an office in Athens where there'll
be papers to sign, and when you come home you'll be
Thíos Dimitri's son; he'll be your father.'

One thing Niki had always wanted was a father, for his
natural father had never acknowledged him as his son,
and it was something Niki had always missed, especially
after he started school. 'You mean I shall have a father? A
real *father*?' His huge eyes glowed with excitement as the
full meaning of adoption dawned on him at last. 'Does it
really mean that, Carey?'

'That's what it means.'

'But when? When?'

'Not very long now.' His excitement was hard to contain
and it brought a lump to her throat. She felt she could
forgive Dimitri anything as long as he made Niki as happy
as he was at that moment, and she clasped his hands
tightly. 'You'll like that, won't you, darling?'

He nodded enthusiastically, but something evidently
still puzzled him for he eyed her thoughtfully for a
moment. 'Will I be getting a new mother too?' he asked,
and Carey wondered if she could answer that with any
certainty.

She had heard nothing about Dimitri having plans to
marry, and she felt sure she'd have heard about it if there
had been, from Mitso if from no-one else. Nevertheless she
dealt with it cautiously. 'Well now, I can't really say for
certain about that, Niki, but I wouldn't think so.'

'But Thíos Dimitri hasn't got a mother?'

Carey understood him well enough not to take the
question at face value, and she shook her head. 'He isn't
married as yet, so I shouldn't think you'll be getting a
new mother right away.'

Obviously relieved, Niki sighed. 'Good, then I can

still have you, can't I?'

The matter of her returning home hadn't cropped up for some time now, but the way things were going Carey wondered if it might not be as well to put the idea in Niki's mind that she wouldn't always be there. Sooner or later Dimitri was going to decide that she had served her purpose and send her back, and while he was still happy about getting a father, it might be a good time to let Niki know it.

He had settled well into his new school and language was proving less of a barrier every day, thanks to Dimitri's infinite patience and tutoring. Even the family seemed to have relaxed their attitude towards him lately, and he already seemed very much more Greek than the little boy she had brought from England a couple of months ago, so it might be a good time.

'Niki,' she held his hands but found it hard to meet those big ingenuous eyes while she told him, 'now that you're to have a father of your own and you've settled so well here, you wouldn't mind too much if I had to go away, would you?' He was frowning, she noticed from the corner of her eye, and it was clear that she had misjudged his reaction, but there was no chance of her going back now. 'You're getting to be a big boy, and you have Yayá Karamalis and Thíos Dimitri to look after you, you don't really need me.'

Whatever advantages she reeled off, nothing could alter the fact that she had said she was going away, and Niki was looking at her anxiously. 'You want to go, Carey?'

Those big, solemn eyes had always been very hard to resist, and never more so than now. It was going to be no easier now than it would have been at the beginning, she realised, and she was going to have to harden her heart when it came to the point, however hard it was. 'It isn't up to me,' she explained. 'I work for your Thíos Dimitri, Niki.'

But Niki wasn't concerned with things like that, he was

simply unhappy about the idea of her leaving him. 'Don't
you like it here?" he asked, and Carey didn't see how she
could avoid a full-scale explanation, for Niki was
Karamalis enough to make evasion difficult if not impossible.

'It isn't a question of my liking it or not,' she told him,
'it's a matter of whether or not your uncle considers I'm
still needed her. You see, I'm not Greek like you are and I
don't really belong here, so sooner or later I shall have to
leave and go back to England. I can't *really* stay for ever,
darling, that was never on the books.'

'Why?'

Only a moment since Carey had been hoping that no one
would come to interrupt them, now she heaved a sigh of
thankfulness when she spotted Dimitri coming across the
patio towards them. It was seldom that she found herself
at a loss with Niki, but this time she simply didn't feel she
could give him the answer he wanted, and having Dimitri
join them was one way of avoiding further questions.

Dark slacks and a white shirt made the most of his
almost primitive virility and his darkness, and she felt the
inevitable flutter of sensation that he always caused. Even
though it was weeks since that eventful visit to the temple
of Artemis, and nothing had happened between them since
then, she could still feel a thrill of pleasure at the remembered touch of his hands and the ravishment of that
fierce mouth. It was something she could never be sure
she regretted or not, but it was something she could never
forget.

'Thíos Dimitri is coming,' she told Niki. 'Don't forget to
tell him how excited you are that he's going to become
your *papá*, will you?'

Niki was leaning against her chair and eyeing his uncle
thoughtfully. 'I shall tell him that he's got to 'dopt you
too,' he announced with a definite hint of the Karamalis
arrogance, and it was too late by then for Carey to attempt
to dissuade him.

One thing that had changed since the visit to the temple was that Dimitri now called her by her first name, and he was perhaps a little more relaxed in her company, particularly if Niki was with them. Perhaps because he was suddenly feeling a little shy about the coming change in their relationship, Niki was less uninhibited in his welcome than he usually was, and Dimitri must have noticed it, for he glanced at Carey and raised a brow—probably suspecting that she had made less of a success of breaking the news than he hoped.

He murmured a greeting, then stretched himself out in the chair beside hers, and she took the increased urgency of her heartbeat as inevitable, like the flush in her cheeks and a curious little catch in her voice when she answered him. However long she remained under his roof she would never be able to simply accept Dimitri as she did the rest of his family. Not for anything would she admit to falling in love with him, and sometimes when the symptoms seemed to point that way, she quickly subdued them.

'Yássu!' He greeted Niki in Greek as he always did now, and reached out a hand to him. 'I thought I would find you out here. Tell me,' he said, drawing him close beside him, 'what have you and Carey been talking about, eh?'

'I've told him——' Carey began, but Dimitri waved her to silence with a touch of his more usual asperity.

'Nikolas will tell me himself, will you not?'

Uncertain, Niki gave her a swift glance from the corner of his eye, but he was much less in awe of his once-feared uncle now, and he stood with one hand on the arm of Dimitri's chair and the other rubbing back and forth over his own thick black hair. 'Carey says that you're going to be my father and you're going to—to 'dopt me.'

'I am going to adopt you, Nikolas. Do you know what it means?'

'That you'll sign some papers and when we come home you'll be my father.' His excitement at the prospect was rekindled and his eyes glowed darkly as he looked at the man who was soon to become so very much more important to him. 'I never had a father; are you really going to be my father, Thíos Dimitri?'

'That is right.'

'And will I call you Father or Thíos Dimitri? I'd much rather call you Father.'

Seeing the sudden look of pleasure on Dimitri's face came as a surprise to Carey and set her wondering if he really was adopting Niki simply from a sense of duty. 'I would rather that you called me either Papá or Patéras, you may choose.'

'Papá.' Niki tried it and liked it. 'Papá, Papá, Papá!'

Dimitri put a finger over his mouth to stem his enthusiasm, but it was quite clear that he was pleased about it, and the rapport that had been growing between them over the past weeks seemed to have reached a new high in this moment of excitement. 'It will please you to have a *papá*, eh?'

Niki beamed. 'Oh yes!' Then he sobered again in one of the lightning changes of mood that had always intrigued Carey and reminded her of his mother. 'Are you going to—adopt Carey too so that she can't go back to England?'

She caught her breath, her heart clamouring wildly as Dimitri turned and regarded her steadily for a moment. 'Does Carey speak of going back to England?' he asked, and Niki nodded, frowning at the idea.

'I don't think she *wants* to go, but she says she works for you and you have to say. But if you adopt her too then she can't go, can she?'

On the surface Dimitri seemed to be treating the subject as seriously as Niki did, and he pondered for a moment before he replied. 'It is not possible for anyone to adopt a grown woman, even if Carey was willing,' he explained carefully to Niki. 'You see, when one is of age—grown up?—one has a free choice, and if Carey wishes to return to England there is nothing I can do to prevent it, but perhaps we can think of something that might persuade her, eh?'

So he meant to throw the onus on to her, Carey thought, and looked at him reproachfully, for it was because he had been so insistent that she stayed in the first place that she was still there. Also this half-joking mood was something new to her, and she wasn't quite sure how to react to it. 'If I remember correctly,' she ventured, 'I wasn't given a choice when I first came here. You informed me that I was staying, and that was it, my opinion didn't enter into it!'

'But you stayed,' Dimitri's shiveringly soft voice pointed out. 'In fact I could have done nothing to prevent you leaving at any time you chose; the way was open to you, you were not kept here by force, yet you stayed. Does that not suggest to you that you had no real wish to leave, Carey?'

Her hands were shaking so much that she gripped the arms of her chair tightly. To think of him having even an inkling of her disturbed and tangled emotions where he was concerned appalled her, and her mind turned again to that fateful Saturday when he had volunteered to drive her to the temple of Artemis in Mitso's place. Whatever happened she treasured those few moments of wild abandon as she did no other moment in her life, and for the moment even Niki had been put to the back of her mind and half forgotten.

'You don't know how hard it was for me to go; to say on any particular day, this is the day I'll leave, I'm no longer needed here.' She moistened her lips with a flick of her tongue and wished her voice sounded less unsteady. Why could she never talk to him as she would have done to anyone else? 'You don't know how——'

'I can guess,' Dimitri assured her quietly. 'But you have no need to make excuses for remaining. If you feel you must justify your being here, Nikolas still needs you; even though he will soon have a father it will not, I think, entirely compensate for losing you, and I wish him to be happy.'

He had chosen a roundabout and rather non-committal way of saying it, but Carey thought he was asking her to stay on, living there and caring for Niki, and he must have a fair idea of how much she wanted to do just that. 'You—you're asking me to stay on after the adoption goes through?'

Still he didn't give her a straightforward answer, but looked to Niki to do it for him. 'You would like that, would you not, Nikolas?'

He had no real need to ask Niki's opinion, and he was left in no doubt of it when Niki climbed up on to her lap and threw his arms about her neck, planting a noisy and affectionate kiss on her cheek. 'You stay,' he declared. 'Thíos Dimitri says so!'

Which was exactly what had happened at the beginning, Carey thought, only in this instance she was much more willing to comply; and not only for Niki's sake either.

The following morning when Dimitri announced that he was taking Niki to visit a nearby beach it was taken for granted that Carey would go with them. She wasn't consulted, but by now she hardly expected to be where Dimitri was concerned. Nor did she possess a swimsuit, but as she told Niki, it didn't really matter because she would be quite happy just sitting on the beach and watching the two of them.

Niki had gone with Dimitri to fetch the car round, and Carey found herself in the *salon* with most of the Karamalis family, and she was aware of Rhoda Karamalis watching her from the corner of her eye. 'I suppose you are to go with them to care for the child,' she said after a few moments. She never referred to Niki as anything other than the boy, or the child, and Carey took note of the glint in her eyes and the note of sarcasm in the heavily accented voice. 'The new *papá* is perhaps not so very sure of himself, eh?'

Her abrupt spurt of laughter brought colour to Carey's cheeks, but she managed to answer coolly enough. 'Oh, I don't think it's that, Kyria Karamalis,' she told her. 'Niki and his uncle are very good friends.'

She wished Rhoda did not show her dislike of the two of them quite so obviously; not for her own sake so much as for Niki's. But in this instance support came from a quite unexpected quarter. Minerva Thoulou, the sober widowed sister, was selecting a magazine from those on a nearby table, giving her attention to what she was doing and not looking at Carey even when she spoke.

'You are accustomed to children, Thespinís Gordon, and my brother is not, it is sensible to have you accompany them. And also perhaps Nikolas would not care to go without you.'

Both her speech and her understanding were a revelation to Carey, who had never heard her say more than a dozen words in English the whole time she had been there. She didn't offer any other encouragement, but Carey felt that was good enough for the moment, though she noticed how Rhoda frowned at her sister-in-law.

'You're probably right on both counts, Kyria Thoulou, and I'm certainly not averse to a morning by the sea, I haven't seen the sea for years.'

Whether or not Minerva would have grasped the opportunity to continue the conversation, Carey was never to know, for Rhoda Karamalis took a hand once more and there was a faint, derisive curl on her full lips that no one could miss. 'Who would concern themselves with that when they live in London?' she asked. 'I shall not trouble myself if I never see the sea again when I live there!'

Carey had heard nothing about Andoni and his family visiting England, and it struck her as curious, for Mitso would surely have told her if it was general knowledge. Ignoring the way it was said, Carey took the statement at face value in an attempt to bridge what had so far been an unbridgeable gap between them. 'I didn't know you were going to live in London, Kyria Karamalis, how exciting. Where abouts will you be staying?'

It was debatable how far Rhoda would have been prepared to confide in her, but in the event she was given no opportunity, for Andoni lowered his newspaper and frowned discouragingly at his wife, at the same time speaking rapidly and firmly in their own tongue. Rhoda shrugged, but her look was as sulky as a spoiled child's and Carey wondered what was in the air that Andoni Karamalis did not want talked about.

It was with the idea of easing the uneasy silence that followed that she turned once more to Minerva Thoulou and picked up the original subject. 'I don't think I could ever get blasé about the sea, I love it too much. To me it's always exciting, and I can sit and just look at it for hours and never get bored. It has a very special appeal, don't you think so, Kyria Thoulou?'

Minerva selected her magazine and she folded it carefully into her hand before she replied, quietly and without expression, as she always did, her eyes downcast. 'I am afraid I do not share your view, Thespinis Gordon. Please excuse me.'

She walked with her usual easy grace across the room, and as she watched her close the door behind her Carey remembered, and her heart beat quickened in dismay. Aliki had told her once about Minerva having married very young and been widowed only weeks later when her husband was drowned while they were out together in their sailing dinghy. She couldn't imagine how she could have been so tactless, nor did she know quite what to do about it.

Turning, she noticed the unmistakable curl on Rhoda's lip, and the way her son Damon's eyes gleamed as he looked at her. There was no hint of pity in either of them, and Carey moistened her lips anxiously. 'I—I can't think how I could have forgotten how her husband died,' she

VISIT 4 MAGIC PLACES FREE

ISTANBUL

BEYOND THE SWEET WATERS by Anne Hampson
The brooding yet lovely Jeanette vowed never to love another man after the tragic death of her fiancé. But mysterious Istanbul and the proudly handsome archaeologist were threatening to be too much for her to resist.

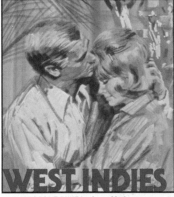

WEST INDIES

THE ARROGANT DUKE by Anne Mather
A new life, a hidden identity on an idyllic Caribbean island....Was it all for naught just because the passionate, arrogant duke chose to believe a vicious lie about her? Juliet feared the worst.

LADRANA

TEACHERS MUST LEARN by Nerina Hilliard
Would Laurel, the beautiful but inexperienced schoolteacher, really learn the true meaning of love on the exotic island of Ladrana? Or would her engagement to wealthy Stephen Barrington prove only to be a cruel charade?
Ladrana: a small Portuguese island off the coast of East Africa.

CALIFORNIA

CAP FLAMINGO by Violet Winspear
Fern was beautiful, sensitive and vulnerable. What she really needed now was some kindness and understanding...not a loveless marriage to an egotistical journalist, a situation that could only lead to more heartbreak and unhappiness.

A HARLEQUIN ROMANCE:

You don't just read it. You live it...

Harlequin Romances are the ultimate in romantic fiction, the kind of stories you can't put down. They are stories full of the adventures and emotions of love... full of the hidden turmoil beneath even the most innocent-seeming relationships. Desperate clinging love, emotional conflict, bold lovers, destructive jealousies and romantic imprisonment – you'll find them all in the passionate pages of **Harlequin Romances**.

Let your imagination roam to the exotic reaches of the world. Meet true-to-life people. Become intimate with those who live larger than life. **Harlequin Romances** are the kind of books you just can't put down... the kind of experiences that remain in your dreams long after you've read about them.

4 FREE BOOKS FOR YOU

Mail to Harlequin Reader Service

YES, please send me FREE and without obligation my 4 **Harlequin Romances**. If you do not hear from me after I have examined my 4 FREE books, please send me the 6 new **Harlequin Romances** each month as soon as they come off the presses. I understand that I will be billed only $9.00 for all 6 books. There are no shipping and handling nor any other hidden charges. There is no minimum number of books that I have to purchase. In fact, I can cancel this arrangement at any time. The first 4 books and the tote bag are mine to keep as FREE gifts, even if I do not buy any additional books.

CR174

NAME   (please print)

ADDRESS   APT. NO.

CITY   STATE/PROV.   ZIP/POSTAL CODE

If under 18, parent or guardian must sign.

This offer is limited to one order per household and not valid to present subscribers. If price changes are necessary you will be notified. Offer expires Sept. 30, 1982.

PRINTED IN U.S.A.

murmured. 'Perhaps if I go after her and——'

'What use would that be?' Rhoda demanded, and Carey shook her head.

'If only I'd thought before I spoke!'

'If only you had, *thespinís*!' Rhoda's dark eyes gleamed with malice. 'My husband and his brothers are very fond of Minerva, and Dimitri especially so.'

Carey could imagine all sorts of repercussions from her one innocuous question, and she stood for a moment trying to think of ways of making amends, if indeed there was any. Then she became aware, vaguely, of a car stopping outside, and a moment after that Niki's voice calling to her. 'Carey! Carey, come on!'

She hesitated, and the look in Rhoda's eyes did nothing to reassure her. 'Should you not go, *thespinís*?' she suggested with feline softness. 'Dimitri does not like to be kept waiting.'

Outside Niki's voice was again urging her to hurry, and after a moment's hesitation she turned swiftly and went hurrying out of the room. The door was not quite closed behind her when she heard Rhoda's short, malicious laugh again, and it lent speed to her departure.

Niki was already half-way up the steps on his way to fetch her when she appeared, and he grabbed her hand and pulled her along after him, chattering excitedly and scolding her for keeping them waiting. 'Thíos Dimitri will go without you if you don't hurry up,' he informed her, and seeing Dimitri sitting there and tapping his long fingers impatiently on the steering wheel Carey could well believe it.

As she slid into the seat beside him she gave him a brief sidelong glance but offered no reason for the delay, only an apology. 'I'm sorry to have kept you waiting,' was all she said, and Dimitri turned and gazed at her for a moment, his eyes on her down-turned mouth.

'What is wrong, Carey?'

It was inevitable, Carey told herself, that her expression

would give her away, and Dimitri was adept at noticing things like that. But she wasn't inclined to tell him how tactless she had been with his sister at the moment, and she turned her head aside and looked out of the window, making it clear that she had no intention of satisfying him.

'Nothing!' she said shortly.

She could feel the intensity of his gaze, but she kept her head determinedly averted until he gave up. 'As you wish,' he said quietly and with a slight shrug, but as he set the car in motion there was something in his manner that got to Carey.

She had not intended to snub him quite so definitely and she already regretted it, so that she acted on impulse as she so often did; looking at him earnestly as she sought to explain. 'I'm sorry. It's just that I've just been un-forgivably tactless and said something to Kyria Thoulou that I'd never have dreamed of saying if I'd thought first. I should have remembered that she wouldn't like anything to do with the sea after her husband was drowned.'

They drove down the tree-lined private road and on to the public road before Dimitri gave her his attention again, and his quiet way of speaking suggested he took the fact of her tactlessness much less seriously than she did herself. 'What exactly did you say to Minerva?' he asked.

'I—I asked her if she didn't love the sea as much as I do. It was horribly thoughtless of me and I do hope she doesn't think I did it deliberately.'

'Minerva has far too much sense to do that,' Dimitri assured her confidently. 'It is nine years since Konstandi Thoulou was drowned and Minerva is probably unaware that you know how he died.'

'Aliki told me.'

'Ah yes.' He nodded as if it was what he expected. 'Did Minerva appear upset?'

When she thought about it, Carey couldn't honestly say that Minerva had seemed upset; she had merely replied that she did not share her view, that was all. 'Not really,'

she said. 'It was Kyria Karamalis who seemed to think I'd
upset her, after Kyria Thoulou had gone.' She sighed and
gave him a very wan smile when he half turned his head
for a moment. 'It doesn't seem to be my day, in fact,
although it wasn't me who originally mentioned London,
it was Kyria Karamalis. She said something about not
missing the sea when she lived in London and I merely
asked where they would be staying while they were there.
Then your brother Andoni stepped in and seemed
annoyed with her because she'd mentioned it at all.'

'So Rhoda spoke of living in London, eh?'

Something about the way he asked made her turn her
head and frown at him curiously. 'Just that—that she
wouldn't miss the sea when she went to live there.'

'Ah!'

There was a faint half-smile on his lips for a moment
that puzzled her, for it didn't strike her that he was particularly amused, but he said no more on the subject, and
gradually Carey began to give her attention to the
countryside instead. They drove through the now familiar
vineyards and olive groves for the most part, fresh bright
countryside that gave occasional glimpses of some ruined
temple high on a wooded hillside and recalled another,
very different, outing with Dimitri.

In the back seat Niki was chattering away happily about
what they were going to do, and how his uncle was going
to teach him to swim, and it gave Carey a quite unexpected thrill of pleasure when Dimitri caught her eye
briefly and smiled. It was a small, secret smile that suggested intimacy, and aroused a response from her impres-
sionable senses that she found hard to control.

Then suddenly they were turning off the main highway
and on to a narrower, rougher-surfaced road at right
angles to it, with trees growing on both sides and seeming
to lead nowhere but into the broad sweep of the sky. Just
as when they had stood in the little temple of Artemis,
Carey had a feeling of being on the very edge of eternity,

and her heart was already beating with the urgency of anticipation.

Then, just when it seemed they must go plunging into nothingness, Dimitri made a swift left-hand turn and braked the car to a halt, and when she had grown accustomed to the quiet Carey could just make out the unmistakable sound of the sea. Dimitri sat for a moment with an arm over the steering-wheel, looking down at the dazzling blue lift of the sky, then he turned to warn Niki to stay where he was. 'From here we have to walk,' he said.

Carey was already reaching for the door handle when Dimitri leaned across to do it for her, and the pressure and warmth of his body again brought those disturbing recollections to mind, so that she leaned as far back in her seat as she could to try and lessen the contact. Not that it lessened the effect at all, and her pulse was beating so hard it deafened her to everything else when the brush of his hand on her breast aroused all those wild emotions she had thought were firmly under control.

'Do not attempt to go down without me.'

The warning was spoken close to her mouth and his eyes burned straight into hers, as if he suspected she would do almost anything to avoid contact with him, but she shook her head. 'I—I won't,' she promised.

Stepping out into the cool fresh air, she tipped back her head and let the wind blow on to her flushed cheeks, while some small traitorous thought briefly wished that Niki need not have come with them. Such was the effect Dimitri had on her, and she shook her head dismissively when she realised the direction her thoughts were taking. Rhoda and Minerva had been right, he had brought her to take care of Niki and for no other reason.

Niki came bounding up to her the moment Dimitri let him out of the car and, because of the way her mind had been working, Carey hugged him for a moment to convince herself she hadn't really wanted to come without him. He looked up at her and grinned, his dark eyes sparkling and happy. 'I'm glad you came too, Carey.'

There appeared to be nothing beyond the edge of the ridge of grass-grown rocks, but a moment later they stood looking down at a scene that took her breath away. The land sloped sharply in massive cliffs, tree-covered but apparently quite negotiable and by way of a wide path that wound all the way down to a small sandy cove and the rich, amethyst blue waters of the Aegean gleaming in the sun.

'It's beautiful, just—beautiful.'

It was much the same reaction she had expressed on that last occasion, and she saw the way Dimitri's mouth curved briefly into a smile. 'We shall make a Greek of you yet, Carey,' he said, and Niki laughed.

'Carey can't be Greek, Thíos Dimitri, she's English!'

Dimitri took his hand and began the walk down, which was less hazrdous than Carey had feared, and Carey saw him lower one eyelid briefly. 'We shall see,' he told him, *sotto voce.*

Niki giggled, holding tightly to his hand, and again Carey wondered at the rapport between them. It was a wonderful thing from Niki's point of view, but it did sometimes make her feel rather superfluous, and set her wondering again why Dimitri was so insistent that she stayed.

The cove was bigger than it had looked from above, but it was completely deserted except for themselves, and looking around her Carey sighed contentedly. 'This is perfect,' she said, 'and there isn't a soul in sight.'

'That is the way I prefer it.' Dimitri stood beside her, breathing a little more rapidly than normal, as she was herself, and together they watched Niki run to the water's edge and stand gazing at the sea. It was only moments later that Dimitri realised she was carrying only an ordinary small handbag, and he frowned. 'Did you not bring a swimsuit with you?'

She shrugged, dismissing it as unimportant. 'I haven't one, but it doesn't really matter because I can't swim anyway. I'll be quite happy sitting and watching you two, don't worry.'

'You should have said before we left that you did not have a costume,' he said, and Carey found it hard to believe it was as important to him as he made it sound. 'You could have borrowed one.'

'But I really don't mind,' she insisted.

He glanced across at Niki, then half turned to face her, his expression serious and a faint frown still between his brows. 'Carey—you are not still disturbed by that conversation with Minerva earlier, are you? You do not feel that you have upset her or that she will blame you?'

It wasn't what she expected him to talk about, and Carey took a moment to think. 'I don't think she was now I think about it,' she told him. 'It was Rhoda—Kyria Karamalis who suggested she was, but I'm sorry I said it, whether Kyria Thoulou took offence or not.'

He nodded, and something in the black eyes that watched her sent little shivers of anticipation running along her spine; then he reached out one hand as if to touch her face, seemed to change his mind, and drew back. While she stood trembling, he turned swiftly and looked across at Niki again. 'Can Nikolas swim?' he asked.

Hastily bringing herself back to earth, Carey shook her head. 'He was learning at school, but they'd only got as far as learning to float when he left.'

'Hmm.' She got the feeling that she was in some way held responsible for Niki's lack of prowess, but after a moment he turned and called to him. Partly in Greek and partly in English, as he often did. 'Nikolas, *áz páme!* Collect your swimming trunks and we will go behind those rocks and change.'

Carey noted how obediently Niki came running to collect his things from Dimitri, and as she watched the two of them walking together across the sandy beach, she told herself it was the best possible situation from Niki's point of view. She wasn't really jealous because she was becoming less important to him than she had once been.

Sitting in the shadow of the cliffs it was pleasantly cool and she could see them splashing about at the edge for a while, until apparently Dimitri decided that it was time for a serious swimming lesson. She no longer doubted his patience as she had once done, nor his suitability to handle Niki, and she was quite happy to trust him, even though the vastness of the Aegean seemed to dwarf even his impressive height.

It was unconscious in the first place when her gaze stayed for longer on Dimitri; watching his tall, bronzed body in brief white trunks, his broad shoulders and chest and gleaming, muscular back. She noted the strong arms that had once held her so tightly she had felt she might never breathe again, and had not cared whether or not she did in that moment of ecstasy. When he flung back his head she saw a shower of spray fly from his hair and noticed that it curled slightly when it was wet. He was an earthy, sensual man who could touch her emotions more deeply than anyone ever had before, and the realisation disturbed her strangely.

Sitting there hugging her knees, she felt quite safe studying him as she was, because he could have no idea what she was doing and she could allow her mind to wander along so far unexplored paths, indulging in the kind of daydreams she had never allowed herself before. In fact she became so deeply engrossed that it was a moment or two before she realised the swimming lesson was over and that Niki was being led out of the water.

From where she sat it looked as if he was being told either to dry himself and dress, or to play on the sand, for she saw him nodding his head and a moment later Dimitri was wading out into deeper water again. Like Niki, she watched him until he was no more than an occasional glimpse of bronzed arm flashing upwards, a minute speck of black head on the vastness of the ocean.

Niki had been standing straight-backed and with one hand shading his eyes, the other on his hip and his feet planted firmly apart on the hot sand, but then heaven knew what possessed him. Carey got quickly to her feet when she saw him turn and run back into the water, and she went racing down to the beach when he seemed to disappear suddenly.

'Niki!'

Her heart seemed to be bursting out of her body as she ran, and when she spotted him suddenly she redoubled her effort, for he seemed to be a frighteningly long way out and floating like a small brown cork on the heaving surface of the sea. She called again, but he couldn't have heard her or he would have been bound to respond to the agony in her voice; instead he bobbed on the water, getting farther and farther away from her with every pull of the tide.

'Niki!'

Fully dressed and heedless of the fact that she couldn't swim a stroke, she plunged into the water, fighting for a foothold on the shifting sand, and in the same moment Niki bobbed upright and began to dog-paddle, shouting something she couldn't hear. Her dress dragged at her legs and she wished she had stopped to take that off at least, but she was too busy trying to keep Niki in sight to pay it too much attention.

Then the shelving beach fell away under her feet suddenly and she felt the chill of panic when she realised how completely helpless she was. The sea was calm enough, but her limbs felt as heavy as lead as she scrabbled wildly for some kind of support, gasping for breath when a wave lapped right over her and momentarily forced her under.

Another followed and another, and vaguely it dawned on her that she was on the verge of drowning because she simply hadn't the skill to help herself. She felt heavy and

slow and she couldn't move her limbs at all. As she opened
her mouth to call to Niki again her head felt suddenly
filled with a rush of bright red that seemed to flow right
over her until she lost consciousness.

For some time before she opened her eyes, Carey was
hazily conscious of a sequence of sounds, and of one sound
in particular, like a deep, heavy breathing that was somehow connected with her own breath rhythm. Her heart
felt as if it was pounding away for dear life, and as she
began to remember and panic, another mouth was pressed
firmly over hers and the force of a deep warm breath
entered her lungs and shuddered through her whole body.

She stirred, turning her head from side to side and
making a small whimpering sound of protest, and something beside her moved. A voice, barely above a whisper
and speaking in Greek, breathed words that sounded very
much like a prayer. Then she opened her eyes and found
Dimitri on his knees beside her, his dark features looking
like chiselled bronze and gleaming wetly with sea water.

Carey looked up at him for a long breathless moment,
trying to believe the look of stark relief in his eyes, then
she took a long shuddering breath of her own volition and
turned her head. 'Niki?' she whispered hoarsely, and
turned to look up at him again when his voice grated
harshly.

'I have sent him to sit by himself!'

'He—he's not hurt?' Her throat felt so horribly rough
that it was difficult to speak clearly, and she was anxious
about Niki now because of the fierce look in Dimitri's
eyes. The tip of her tongue flicked quickly over her lips
and she looked at him appealingly. 'Where is he?'

'He has been told to dry himself and get dressed and
then sit on the other side of the rock,' Dimitri informed
her. 'If he has disobeyed me a second time he will be very
sorry!'

It was incredible how lethargic she felt, and it seemed

not to matter that she still lay back on the sand, or that her wet clothes clung to her too closely, the skirt ruckled up around her thighs. She kept thinking about Dimitri's mouth on hers, breathing life back into her, when she knew she should have been more concerned with Niki and what was likely to happen to him for disobeying his uncle.

'He—he was being daring,' she whispered, her grey eyes pleading for understanding. 'Boy-like, he had to prove to himself that he was safe in the water without help.'

'He was disobedient,' Dimitri insisted firmly, and with a look in his eyes that resented her implied criticism. 'Disobedience of this kind calls for punishment, and Nikolas is being punished!'

It was weakness, she knew, but there were tears in her eyes as she looked up at him and she seemed not to be able to do anything about them. 'Don't be too hard,' she begged in the same small, uncertain voice. 'He's very little and he didn't do anything so very awful really.'

'*Théos mou!*' Dimitri breathed, his eyes blazing. 'He could have been drowned himself on that outgoing tide, and you *were* very nearly drowned trying to bring him back! What must he do in your opinion before he deserves punishment?' Tears ran down her cheeks, but she said nothing. Then she heard him murmur in Greek again and he sat back on his heels looking down at her fiercely. 'He has been made to sit alone, out of sight—what is so very terrible about that, eh? Would you make me seem a monster who beats little children? Would that better suit your conception of me?'

'No.'

Her voice was no more than a whisper, and she closed her eyes to try and prevent any more tears from falling. She wasn't used to feeling so weak, and it alarmed her, particularly in the present situation. Dimitri, it seemed, could affect her even when she had been half drowned and was shaking in every limb from shock. A long gentle finger lifted a tear from her cheek and she caught her breath as she turned her head away.

The same fingers brushed back the clinging strands of hair from her neck and there was nothing else she could do but turn her cheek to them, while her breathing deepened to a laboured, exaggerated movement of her breast. Niki sitting alone behind the rock slipped from her mind when Dimitri curved a hand about her cheek, and when he slipped his other hand behind her and raised her from the ground it was instinctive to turn her face to the broad nakedness of his chest.

His skin was cool and damp and the black hair that covered it roughened with salt water so that it prickled her cheek. Then he murmured something in his own tongue and she felt the merest touch of his lips on her forehead. The need to reach up and touch him was irresistible, and she just lightly brushed her fingertips on his shoulder, feeling the slight flinch he gave.

Her hand opened and pressed, flat-palmed, to the pulsing warmth of him, and he murmured something very low and soft as he grasped her upper arms and drew her to him. Yet again it was instinct alone that sparked off her response, and Carey lifted her mouth to him, soft and vulnerable, the lips parted in an invitation he made no attempt to resist.

The hard passionate mouth sought hungrily for her response, burying itself deep in hers, while his arms pressed her with urgent desire to a fiery masculinity barely disguised by the brief costume he wore. Carey sank back on to the ground and his weight forced her deeper into the shifting sand, then she reached up her arms and wound them around his neck.

It was as if she had been cut off from all reality, and she felt the eager response of her own body as something she had no control over, her clinging wet clothes further disrupted by hands that pushed away the thin material while he pressed his mouth to her shoulder and the soft, damp skin of her neck. It was like being on the brink of oblivion, and Carey would have sunk into it willingly in another moment if a small and very uncertain voice had not recalled her.

'Carey—you all right?'

Her own response was a dazed kind of guilt, but Dimitri's was passion, fierce and unrelenting. He raised himself with incredible speed and a moment later stood towering over both her and Niki, his black eyes blazing. Niki stood his ground, but he rubbed one hand on his bottom as if he anticipated a smacking, there was a definite quiver about his lower lip that made him look irresistibly appealing, and Carey prayed that Dimitri would find it so too.

Sitting up, she did her best to appear normal, but it was difficult when her head was still spinning and her senses still dazed from Dimitri's kisses. 'I'm all right, Niki, thank you.' She didn't overdo the smile in case Dimitri took it amiss, but she did reach for Niki's hand and hold it tightly. 'It was very wrong of you to go back into the water, you know, and if it hadn't been for your uncle I would have drowned coming in after you. You must promise me never to do anything so silly again.'

His lip still quivered and a quick glance at Dimitri's angry face made him bite into it. 'I promised Thíos Dimitri,' he told her, looking so contrite that she longed to hug him. 'He said you were nearly dead because I didn't do as he said, and if I did anything like that again he'd beat me till I learned.'

With a protest on her lips, Carey looked up at the towering Nemesis above her, but there was challenge enough in his eyes to make her look away again hastily. He was responsible for making Niki behave and he had lacked a man's guidance for too long; also she could not forget that he had been as angry on her behalf as on Niki's—frightened in case he could not breathe life back into her, and fear was not a sensation Dimitri was likely to be very familiar with.

Looking at Niki, she squeezed his hand. 'Then you'd better be a good boy from now on, hadn't you?'

Obviously puzzled, Niki regarded her for a moment with his head to one side. 'Did it make you come alive again when Thíos Dimitri kissed you?' he asked, and the colour flooded into her face.

She started to get to her feet and at once hard fingers clasped her arm and helped her, so that just for a moment she was again held against the naked warmth of Dimitri's body. She dared not look at him, but gave her attention to Niki. 'There are several ways of saving someone's life when they almost drown,' she told him. 'I think you're a little too young to understand at the moment, Niki.'

He shrugged, his confidence returning. 'I think Thía Minerva got saved,' he said, then hurried on without stopping to explain that rather enigmatic statement. 'Do we have to go home now, Carey, or can we stay here?'

'We go home,' Dimitri told him, before Carey could say anything. 'Carey is wet and uncomfortable and very shaky still and she needs to go home and rest.' Niki looked down in the mouth, but he had been responsible for the way she felt, he had been left in no doubt of that, and he was very fond of her, as his sudden impulsive hug showed. 'I shall make use of Nikolas's towel and you will use mine to do what you can about getting dry,' Dimitri went on. 'Nikolas, *fero petséta mou, parakalo.*'

Niki apparently understood what was required of him, for he went off at once, and Dimitri again turned his black gaze on her. 'I—I'm not all that shaky now,' she told him in a quick breathless voice, but he ignored her protest and she gasped when he slid a hand under her chin and raised it, his eyes moving slowly over her face until they came to rest on her mouth with an intensity that made her shiver.

'You prefer Nikolas to think that I was saving your life when I kissed you?' he asked, and Carey looked up swiftly, wondering exactly what made him ask that.

'Don't you think it's best?' she asked in the same light

and slightly husky voice. 'It will save a lot of questions and—well, the *way* you revived me was very much the same thing, wasn't it?'

He conceded it with a shrug, but he continued to gaze at her, and Carey had never felt more small and vulnerable in her life as she stood there on that quiet little beach with him. His nearness and his nakedness disturbed her alarmingly, and she did not raise her eyes again until he reached out to touch her, then she backed away, prompted by some instinct she did not understand, her heart thudding wildly.

She was conscious of the clinging wetness of her dress and the body it so clearly revealed, and Dimitri was frowning, not in anger but as if something puzzled him. 'You are a confusion to me,' Dimitri confessed with unexpected candour, and a stronger accent than usual. 'You allow me to kiss you, you—respond to my kisses, yet still you do not trust me.'

Carey bit her lower lip anxiously, holding back the words she had on the tip of her tongue, and she was thankful to see Niki on his way back with a towel for her. 'Niki's coming back,' she said, and Dimitri narrowed his eyes for a moment, then turned quickly and walked away from her.

As she watched him go Carey shook her head. She did not for a moment believe he saw those moments of passion as anything but a passing pleasure, and how could she tell him that it was her own wild emotions she did not trust where he was concerned?

CHAPTER SIX

HAVING taken Niki to school as usual, Carey took note of the passenger in the car coming from the other direction. When her own chauffeur drew over to let the other vehicle pass on the narrow access road, she had a good view of Minerva Thoulou and smiled, receiving a grave nod of recognition in return, and the sight of her set Carey musing again about the number of times Minerva seemed to go out lately.

She had her own chauffeur and was quite independent, but Carey found it hard to believe that she went on shopping expeditions as often as she seemed to. Grave, quiet Minerva seemed to have little in common with her volatile family, so it was possible she had friends who were more in tune with her own quiet nature. Carey hoped so, because she liked Minerva as well as she liked any of the Karamalises.

Yesterday, after Carey's near-fatal ducking, Minerva and Madame Karamalis must have learned what happened from Dimitri, for she had said nothing to anyone herself, yet both of them had shown genuine concern for her. She knew that Mitso was curious about it and for that reason she had avoided him, both at lunchtime yesterday and at dinner. This morning she had no doubt he would try again unless she managed to keep out of his way until he left for the city.

It had become a habit, after she returned from taking Niki to school, to sit for a while in the *salon*, which was always deserted at that time of day, and when she had taken her things upstairs she made straight for the *salon*. This morning, however, it definitely wasn't deserted and she stopped some distance short of the door when she heard what sounded like a full-scale family row going on.

She recognised Dimitri's voice and Andoni's, but the
loudest and angriest was unmistakably Rhoda's, shrill and
cracking with fury. Heaven knew what had caused it, but
the anger and violence in the voices she heard was deter-
rent enough to make her decide to return to her own
room instead, and she was half-turned when someone
called to her from the other side of the hall.

'Carey!' Mitso was smiling and obviously uncaring, although he could hear what was going on as well as she
could herself. His only concession was a grimace that
briefly distorted his good looks as he came quickly across
the hall to her. 'Very wise of you not to go in,' he told her.
'Although it will be interesting to see how Rhoda manages
to cope in an outright battle with Dimitri!'

He was so obviously untouched by the quarrel between
members of his family that Carey wondered if he ever
concerned himself with anything but his own enjoyment.
He was only a little less malicious than Rhoda, although
up until now it had suited him not to show that side of
himself too often to Carey.

'Obviously I can't go barging in right in the middle of a
family row,' she told him.

'So why not come for a walk in the garden with me?'
Mitso suggested, then noticed her glance at her watch and
clucked his tongue reproachfully. 'I do not need to leave
yet, not while Dimitri is so involved with Rhoda; he will
not notice whether I am here or in Athens.'

At any other time Carey would automatically turn
down any suggestion that meant her being alone with
Mitso, but she wasn't quite aware of what she was doing
when she nodded agreement, and those raised voices were
oddly disturbing somehow. In the event she allowed herself
to be led out into the sunlit garden, glancing back briefly
over her shoulder when Rhoda's voice rose shrilly again,
audible even from the doorway into the garden.

'Dimitri isn't usually here at this time of day,' she
observed, and Mitso laughed.

'Oh, nothing is as usual this morning, *oréos mou!*' He leaned down and brushed his lips against her cheek. 'You have much to answer for!'

Startled, Carey looked up at him and frowned. '*Me?*'

Mitso was smiling, but that glint of malice lurked still in his eyes as he looked down at her. 'But for you Dimitri would have gone at his customary time, but you were late for breakfast and he was in his study, then he missed seeing you before you took the child to school. He would not leave until he had assured himself that you were suffering no ill-effects from your—accident yesterday. If you had not stayed so long in your bed, my lovely, he would have seen for himself and left as he always does.'

'I—I don't believe you.' Carey wasn't sure whether she did or not, but her heart was doing strange and alarming things as she walked with Mitso beside the pool. 'He saw me at lunch and at dinner yesterday, he knows I'm all right.'

'Ah, but he does not know that you have not had—what is it?—reaction after being almost drowned. And you were very unlike yourself yesterday, Carey.' He held tightly to her arm, drawing her into the shade of an over-hanging acacia and holding her there in front of him while he quizzed her with those faintly mocking eyes. 'I will not let you go, my lovely, until you tell me the whole story; I wish to know exactly what happened when you went with Dimitri to the beach yesterday. You were almost drowned, were you not?'

If she claimed that the incident had been less serious than it had in fact been, she would be belittling Dimitri's efforts to save her, but she did not relish telling Mitso the whole story. She had little doubt that Mitso would have done much the same as Dimitri did, but with Dimitri the effect had been so much more devastating.

'It was all rather—silly really,' she began. 'At least my part in it was silly. Dimitri had told Niki to stay out of the water when his swimming lesson was over, but instead he

went back in, and I panicked. The tide was going out and
Niki can only float as yet and I was so scared with Dimitri
out of earshot, or so I thought, that I went dashing into
the water. I can't swim a stroke, and the result was that
Dimitri had to pull me out.'

'Unconscious?' She nodded, reluctant to acknowledge
her own uselessness. 'And then?' Mitso prompted softly.

Her colour was high and she was so unwilling to go into
details that he was bound to guess the reason, and his dark
eyes were again glinting with malice. 'He—he revived
me.'

'Ah!' He was half smiling, amused by her reticence.
'With the—what you call—kiss of life, eh?'

Flushed and uneasy, Carey glared at him. 'Yes!'

His laughter raised goose-pimples all over her body and
she wished she had the will power to simply turn and
leave him and go back to the house. 'I have no doubt that
he found the experience very enjoyable,' he declared. 'And
in return you told him about Rhoda, eh, my lovely?'

'Rhoda?' Carey stared at him blankly. 'I don't know
what you mean, Mitso.'

'Do you not? I understand that Rhoda was—indiscreet.'

Carey stared at him in growing dismay as the truth
began to dawn, glancing briefly over her shoulder as she
recalled those raised, angry voices in the *salon*. 'Mitso,
what are they quarrelling about back there?'

'Can you not guess?' Mitso teased. 'Dimitri hates to
have family business mentioned outside the family and
Rhoda spoke to you of going to London, I understand.
You in turn passed on the information to Dimitri, and he
is angry because if there is one thing that Dimitri dislikes
it is having—how is it you say it?—having his hand forced.
That is what he sees Rhoda doing when she speaks to you
of actually going to London.'

'But I mentioned it only in passing,' Carey protested,
appalled at the result of her careless talk. 'I didn't do it

with the intention of making trouble!'

He shrugged, as uncaring as ever, obviously, taking her face between his cupped hands and stroking her lips with his thumbs. 'Do not worry about it, my lovely. Rhoda has been trying to break away from the family and have her own house ever since she and Andoni married. She does not share the traditional Greek liking for living *en famille*, and for years she has harried Andoni to buy her a house in town because she hates the quiet of the country. A taste I share with her, I have to admit.'

'Then why——' Carey began, and he shook his head.

'Because Andoni does have the liking for family living. When the London office was opened, Rhoda saw it as the opportunity she had been waiting for, but she had not counted on Dimitri. As the head of the business he decides who goes where, and he not only finds Andoni useful here, he does not consider his English good enough to run the London office.'

'And I started all this,' Carey whispered, aghast at her own indiscretion.

Mitso shrugged. 'You only brought matters to a head,' he told her. 'Sooner or later Rhoda would have made it an issue between her and Dimitri, and of course Damon, now that he is older, supports her in most things. But for this—battle, my lovely, Rhoda will not like you.'

'Rhoda never *has* liked me!' Carey retorted, angrily defensive. 'And how could I be expected to know that Dimitri would make a full-scale family row on the strength of one casual remark?' She stood facing him on the side of the pool, her eyes dark and troubled. 'Oh, Mitso, if I had any sense at all I'd pack my things right now and go back to England. I'm not really needed any longer, and none of your family like me.'

'Oh, Carey!' His smile mocked her self-pity, but he again took her face between his hands and brought his face so close that his mouth almost touched hers. '*I* like you,' he murmured, and tipped up her face, touching her lips with his. 'I like you very much, even though you are so unkind to me; because you are so fair and so pretty, and you look so sad. Smile for me, eh?'

He would have kissed her more firmly, but Carey was too concerned with other things, and she shook her head. 'Please be serious, Mitso!'

'But I am serious,' Mitso assured her, and bent his head again. But as he tried to kiss her she turned her head aside and his fingers pressed cruelly hard into her cheeks.

'Please, Mitso!' She tried to move his hands, but he held her more determinedly than ever and his eyes were gleaming. Mitso didn't like being refused. 'If anyone comes and finds you kissing me,' Carey pointed out despairingly, 'there'll be more trouble. You *are* getting married in less than a fortnight, in case you've forgotten!'

'Huh!' As always he resented being reminded and he forced her to look up at him again. 'You allow Dimitri to kiss you,' he said through tightly clenched teeth. 'And do not deny it, I know Dimitri too well, and I read women too well, *kopéla mou!*'

'I don't deny it!' Carey declared recklessly, 'but Dimitri isn't about to get married! Let me go, Mitso!'

She fought him desperately, but he was determined, and he eventually forced his mouth hard over hers, his hands on her face carelessly hurtful until he slid them down and pulled her close into his arms. He was scarcely less gentle than Dimitri was when he kissed her, but her response to him was quite different. In Dimitri's arms her senses clamoured wildly in excitement at the touch of his hands, and the fierce possession of his mouth. When Mitso kissed her she felt only anger and dislike, and a frantic desire to get away from him.

'No, Mitso!'

Desperately she fought against him, but his eyes gleamed darkly with determination, and there was a wildness in his embrace, as if he meant to have his way, whatever her feelings. Pushing against his chest with both hands, Carey hit him with her clenched fists when he did not yield, panting and determined not to let him kiss her mouth again. Then without stopping to think what she was doing, she raised one foot and brought the heel of her sandal down hard on his foot.

Mitso let out a howl of anguish, but it achieved the effect she wanted, and the moment he eased his hold on her to clasp his injured foot, Carey turned and fled back to the house. She slowed down only when she was almost there, just in case someone came out and saw her. Her face was flushed and she was breathing hard as she walked on shaking legs into the hall, and at that moment Rhoda Karamalis was the very last person she wanted to see.

Quite clearly from the expression on Rhoda's face, she had not come of the exchange very well, and her eyes narrowed when she saw Carey come in. She was shaking with temper when she came out of the *salon*, and her high heels made an angry staccato clicking on the tiled floor as she came across the hall, making a confrontation inevitable.

Carey would not admit to being afraid of her, but she was wary, and already edgy after her encounter with Mitso, so that she eyed Rhoda guardedly. For a split second they faced one another, then Rhoda raised her right hand and swung it unerringly. '*Taraxias!*' she spat harshly between clenched teeth, and the blow to her face caught Carey so much off guard that she tottered backwards a couple of paces and almost fell.

It was all over so quickly, and Rhoda continued on across the hall with Carey staring after her in blank disbelief, too stunned for the moment to do anything but rub a hand over her stinging cheek. It was several seconds before she recovered sufficiently to decide that once and for all she would make up her mind to go.

She had had quite enough of the temperamental Karamalises and she wouldn't put up with them any longer. She felt dismayingly tearful, but it was no use, she must be firm, and she would see Dimitri right away and tell him her decision. Presumably he was till in the *salon*, and she turned in that direction, still rubbing her cheek.

Damon came out, followed closely by his father, and the fact that Andoni looked more upset than angry immediately won Carey's sympathy. She could feel sorry for anyone torn between Rhoda and Dimitri, and that could well have been his situation during that fierce quarrel. Damon needed no one's sympathy, he was too much his mother's son.

She found Dimitri, as she expected, in the *salon*, standing by the window at the far end of the room, and every line of his body betrayed just how angry he still was, so that she hesitated briefly before letting him know she was there. His back was to her and his hands clasped behind him, the white shirt he wore stretched over broad shoulders and showing teak-dark skin through its texture.

Why, Carey thought despairingly as she looked across at him, could she never come near him without every nerve in her body responding with those wild, ungovernable emotions? It made her present task so much more difficult, and she clasped her own hands tightly together as she tried to bring her emotions under control.

'Mr Karamalis,' she ventured, but her voice was thin and much lighter than she anticipated, so that she wondered for a moment if he hadn't heard her.

Then he spoke without turning round, and in a voice that was rough-edged and impatient. 'What must I do, Carey, before you will use my first name?' It was so unexpected that for a moment Carey completely forgot why she was there, and stared at him blankly. Then he turned suddenly and fixed her with fierce black eyes. 'Well?'

She was already feeling shaky and uncertain about what she was going to tell him, and she shook her head vaguely. 'I—I don't know. I suppose, because you're my employer——'

She broke off when an unmistakable look in his eyes

reminded her of kisses that could make her head spin, and the colour flooded into her face. 'You were on first name terms with Aliki when she employed you, were you not? I suppose Mitso is privileged because of his youth?'

'No, of course not!'

In fact it hadn't struck her quite so much before, that there were quite a number of years' difference between Dimitri and Mitso and herself, although she supposed it had made a difference in the beginning. Yet despite the familiarity of first names Mitso had never been so physically close or as intimately involved with her as Dimitri had, and she had never yet called him Dimitri to his face. There was, she saw now, a certain illogicality in calling a man by his formal title when he had kissed her as Dimitri had.

Feeling vaguely lost for a moment, she gazed at him uneasily, and after a moment or two he shook his head, coming across the room to her and murmuring in his own tongue. His anger seemed to have been thrown off, and he looked almost contrite. 'Carey! It is no wonder you look startled, I have no quarrel with you.' He reached out and touched her cheek, his black eyes glowingly warm, so that it made what she had come to say so much harder. 'I don't know what—*taraxias*——'

'Troublemaker,' Dimitri supplied, and from the way he glanced at the closed door, it might be supposed he knew who had used it.

'Appropriate, I suppose,' Carey acknowledged with a faint smile. 'I was indirectly to blame for the quarrel you just had with your brother and his wife. Mitso said it all started because I told you what Rhoda said about living in London, and I'm sorry.'

Dimitri heaved his shoulders in a shrug, resigned rather than careless, she guessed. 'It was bound to happen.'

'But I precipitated it,' Carey insisted. 'I didn't expect you to start a fight with your family on the strength of a casual observation, and I feel awful about it.'

He was looking at her flushed face where, even despite her high colour, it was possible to make out the red marks that Rhoda's fingers had left on her cheek. She half turned her head away, but Dimitri reached out and turned her to face him again, frowning and leaning forward to get a better look, and she recognised the anger behind the shivery quietness of his voice.

'Rhoda?' he demanded, and Carey nodded, very reluctantly. He was swearing under his breath in Greek, and his eyes were blazing. 'I will not let her get away with this!' he declared, and to Carey it seemed he was on the point of going after his sister-in-law there and then, so that she quickly placed a hand on his arm, shaking her head when he looked down at her and frowned.

'Please don't make things any worse between you,' she pleaded. 'It won't do any good to quarrel about it, especially as—well, I've decided to leave here anyway. That was what I came in to see you about.'

Dimitri fixed her with the steady and unwavering gaze that she always found so disturbing, and she kept her eyes downcast rather than look at him. A pulse in his throat beat rapidly and betrayed his emotions more clearly than the look on his face, and Carey watched its wild beat with a kind of hypnotised fascination, not knowing whether she wanted him to accept the situation matter-of-factly, or put obstacles in her way, as he had done before.

'Why?' he asked, and the softness of his voice was something she found hard to cope with.

She simply stood for a moment not knowing how to begin, then she lifted her shoulders in a shrug and shook her head. 'I—I just think the time has come,' she said, hoping the tears that made her voice so small and husky did not break out and undermine her completely. 'I said once, if you remember, that it wasn't easy to just say one day—this is the day, this is when I'm not needed any more, when I should pack up and go home.'

'And you believe you are no longer needed here?'

Carey shook her head, swallowing hard on the tears that brimmed in her eyes. 'Niki is quite at home here now, he depends on you more and more, and he—he doesn't really need me like he did.'

'You think not?'

Carey bit anxiously into her bottom lip. If only he would answer positively instead of countering everything she said with a question! 'You—you're all he needs, especially after you adopt him,' she said. 'He'll have the father he's always wanted——'

'But no mother,' Dimitri pointed out quietly. 'You have made an excellent job of being his mother for more than four years now, and I do not think he will readily let you go; especially after you risked your life for him yesterday.'

'That was something anyone would have done in the same circumstances with a child involved!'

'I disagree,' Dimitri stated firmly. 'It shall be Nikolas who decides when you go.'

'Not you?' Carey queried in a tight little voice. 'The first time you more or less ordered me to stay, and you've talked me out of it a couple of times since then, even though you did put the blame on Niki. I've told you my mind is made up, I don't know why you won't for once just take it as a cut-and-dried fact that I'm leaving!'

She gasped aloud when he slid a hand under her chin and raised her face, and her heart was beating so hard that she breathed quickly and unevenly and with parted lips. 'You wish to go?' Dimitri asked, with the deep softness in his voice that could well be her undoing.

Only in this instance she wasn't going to let herself be swayed. She swallowed hard and she was shaking like a leaf, but she had made up her mind. 'I wish to go,' she insisted huskily. 'I shall go and pack and be away from here before Niki comes home from school. It will be better that way.'

'Indeed you will not.'

He spoke quietly, but with such firmness that Carey

stared at him, and brushed a hand across her eyes so that she could see him better. Staring at him, she flicked an anxious tongue over her lips. 'You—you can't stop me,' she whispered, but looking at Dimitri's face she knew that he could and that he intended to, and there was nothing she could do about the small fluttering pulse in her breast that prayed he would be successful.

'I can demand that you serve a term of notice,' he told her. 'You may leave here in one month's time, Carey, if you still wish to, but not one day sooner!'

Bewildered and feeling strangely lightheaded, Carey shook her head. 'But why?'

She watched him while he bent and took a long black cheroot from a box on one of the tables, watching, fascinated, the movements of long brown fingers and the angle of the dark head bent intently over the task of lighting it. And he did not look at her again until a drift of smoke half concealed his face.

'Because Nikolas must have time to become accustomed to the idea,' he told her, still in the same quiet voice. 'I am sure you see the reason for that, caring for him as you do.'

'I'm probably the only one who does, apart from his grandmother,' Carey remarked bitterly, and she could do nothing about the shivery uncertainty of her voice.

'You assume a great deal, Carey, you always did.' It was hard to believe the compassion she thought she saw in his eyes though a confusing haze of smoke, but his voice affected her as it always did. 'I sometimes wonder what Aliki can have said about me that made you come here with such a unshakeable determination to dislike me.'

'Oh, but I don't dislike you!' She spoke up quickly and without stopping to think about it, and for a moment his black eyes held hers steadily, while he blew a stream of smoke from between pursed lips.

'I had begun to believe so,' he said quietly, and she felt the colour come once more flooding into her cheeks. 'You have been rather less discouraging toward me in certain situations than you are towards my brother.'

'I don't——' Carey began, but he cut her short.

'I think you do, Carey,' he said. 'In less than two weeks' time Mitso is to marry Despina Glezos and he will no longer be living here after that, but meanwhile you would be wiser if you avoided being alone with him as you were today.'

'I do try,' Carey promised, 'but today I—I wasn't thinking very straight, I'd overheard you all quarrelling in here and it worried me, otherwise I wouldn't have gone with him.'

'Let us hope what happened today will deter him at least for a few days,' said Dimitri, and Carey looked at him curiously.

'What happened today?' she asked, and he took her arm, leading her across to the window he had been looking out of when she came into the room.

He pointed a finger and Carey followed its direction and found herself looking along the path that led from the house to the pool and the patio. Because the path itself took a winding course between trees and shrubs it had never occurred to her before that the patio itself, and the poolside, were visible from the *salon* windows. Mitso was gone now, but she could recognise the exact spot where the two of them had stood not ten minutes since, and her heart was thudding anxiously hard as she looked up at Dimitri.

'I—I didn't realise we could be seen,' she said in a small husky voice. 'I know how it must have looked my going out there with him, but I simply didn't stop to think.' She moistened her lips again. 'I hope you don't think I encourage him.'

It seemed so important that he believed her, and as she watched him gouge out his cheroot in an ashtray she noticed he was smilingly faintly. When he looked at her again it was with that curious gentleness he showed sometimes. 'Mitso needs no encouragement,' he told her. 'It is the nature of the Greek male to pursue any pretty woman who takes his fancy and it seldom occurs to him that he will be refused. You must forgive us, Carey.'

'Us?'

At the swift, impulsive question he arched a brow, then looked at the heavy gold watch on his wrist while Carey wished the floor would open up and swallow her. 'If you will excuse me,' Dimitri said, 'I must attempt to catch up on my timetable.' When he leaned forward it seemed he meant to kiss her and Carey's heart jolted wildly into a hard, rapid beat, but instead he looked deeply into her eyes and warmed her lips with his breath when he spoke. 'Will I risk having *my* foot stamped upon if I kiss you?' he asked softly, and when she shook her head, he kissed her very, very gently; not at all as she expected. '*Heréte*, Carey.'

Two weeks had never gone by so quickly, Carey thought, and she found herself somehow involved in the excitement of Mitso and Despina's wedding without really meaning to be. It was simply impossible not to be affected by all the emotional traumas it generated, and the loud and prolonged arguments that went on about things Carey knew nothing about.

Whether or not marriage would make any difference to Mitso's predatory instincts, she didn't attempt to guess, but she doubted if it would deter him altogether, even if it slowed him down a little. Despina was a strong-willed girl, she suspected, and he would need to take heed of her wishes or she would know the reason why.

Also, Carey had learned, Despina's family were in the same line of business as the Karamalises and Despina was an only child, so the marriage would eventually make Mitso a very rich man as well as a powerful and influential one. Just as long as his father-in-law was satisfied with his treatment of his daughter.

Seeing him on his wedding day it was hard to believe that Mitso had ever been a very half-hearted fiancé, but then of course he was at the centre of attention today, and that was where Mitso liked to be. He beamed at everyone, and at none more warmly than his darkly voluptuous Despina, and he seemed perfectly happy to give up his single state, whatever impression he had given beforehand.

As it was Carey's first experience of a Greek wedding, she found it all a bit overwhelming. The excitement it generated amazed her, for it seemed to involve everyone for miles around, and not only the families immediately concerned. People from the surrounding villages came pouring in, along with countless relatives of both the bride and groom; crowding into the church and, afterwards, into the grounds of the Glezos villa for the wedding feast.

The local wines flowed like water and two groups of musicians made sure that there was always music for dancing. Niki was safe enough, playing nearby where Madame Karamalis was sitting, so when Dimitri insisted on her joining in the traditional *kalamatianos* she had no excuse not to go. But willing as she was, her lack of skill and the energy required proved too much and she eventually collapsed with laughter and had to give up.

A chorus of good-natured jibes greeted her withdrawal and as she sat down beside Madame Karamalis the old lady looked at her flushed face and smiled. 'You find our dances too energetic for you, Thespinís Gordon?'

Carey nodded. The laughter in her eyes was bolstered by several glasses of Pallini, and she fanned a cooling hand in front of her face as she replied. 'I'm exhausted, *madame*,' she admitted cheerfully, 'and I've never been so hot in my life, but it was fun.'

'And you are glad Dimitri persuaded you to dance, eh?'

'It was an experience,' Carey agreed, and the wine sparkled in her eyes as she laughed. 'I'd never have had the nerve to try it if Dimitri hadn't shanghaied me, and to be honest I hadn't the nerve to tell him I wouldn't try! But oh, where *do* your people get their stamina from, *madame?*'

Madame Karamalis smiled as at a compliment. 'It is a national characteristic, *thespints*. Our men particularly have great—verve, eh?'

She was looking at Dimitri as she said it, Carey noticed, and found it hard to take her own eyes off him, for she had never seen Dimitri behave quite so uninhibitedly in public before. He was leading one of the circles of dancers in the *kalamatianos*, which meant that he took the most energetic part. Lean and dark as a satyr, he swirled and leapt in the midst of the group, lunging in mock sword-play and seemingly inexhaustible.

'I have to agree,' Carey allowed. There was a great deal of verve in Dimitri's performance, and it was almost impossible for her to look anywhere else but at him.

As more people joined in, a second circle was formed led by Mitso, and although his performance was obviously designed to outdo his brother's, it somehow fell short. He spotted Carey sitting with his mother and left his place as leader to come over to them, his intent made obvious by the look in his eyes. 'Carey, come, you must dance!'

His dark eyes burned with excitement and he was breathing hard as he reached and took her hand, pulling her to her feet even though she shook her head at him. 'I've been dancing,' she protested, 'and I really couldn't try again yet, Mitso, I'm much too hot.'

'Not even for me?' His mouth pursed, and his face came close, flushed and confident and not for a moment believing she would refuse him. He seemed not to even notice that Despina, his new wife, was watching him and frowning, her face flushed below the virginal white veil. 'For me, Carey, yes?' he insisted, but Carey was still shaking her head.

She freed her hand and stepped back from him, and it was a quite unconscious gesture when she looked over at

Dimitri. 'Not at the moment, Mitso, I'm much too hot. I can't keep pace with you all; I was just saying so to Madame Karamalis.'

'You would disappoint me?'

If he was unaware of Despina's eyes on them, he must have been the only one who was, and Carey very pointedly backed still farther away when he attempted to take her hand again. 'I need to take a breather, Mitso, and I think your group is missing you—and your bride.'

Still he stood his ground, unwilling to admit defeat, as always, until Madame Karamalis said something to him, very quietly and in Greek. He looked for a moment as if he might defy even his mother, but then he shrugged his eloquent shoulders and murmuring something under his breath, went back to join his bride and his friends, while Carey heaved a sigh of relief.

Madame Karamalis was watching her with her dark hooded eyes, and it occurred to Carey that she was probably speculating, as Dimitri had done on occasion, just how affected she was by her handsome youngest son. A surprisingly strong hand was pressed over hers suddenly, and Carey turned to look at her.

'You do not care for my son?' Madame Karamalis asked.

Thinking that she knew exactly what she meant by caring for him, Carey gave her head a very definite shake. 'I don't care for him at all in the way you mean, *madame*, please believe me.'

Once more it was quite unconscious when she glanced across at Dimitri, and in this instance Madame Karamalis followed the direction of her gaze, her black eyes thoughtful. 'Ah,' she said softly. 'Then I have no cause to concern myself.'

'None at all,' Carey assured her.

'You have no one?'

Again Carey shook her head. 'No, *madame*.'

'You are a very attractive young woman,' Madame

Karamalis informed her. 'You should have a husband, Thespinís Gordon. It may be that you will find Greek men to your taste, eh?'

It was a subject that Carey found too sensitive to discuss with ease, so she merely smiled. But as she sat watching the dancers, her eyes inevitably followed Dimitri, whirling and leaping with the agility of an acrobat, and she wondered just how aware he was of the number of feminine eyes that followed his performance. He wasn't naïve enough to be unaware of his own appeal to women, but neither did he deliberately seek their admiration as Mitso did, Carey believed. He simply followed his own inclinations and accepted whatever it brought him as a matter of course.

Watching him, she felt a sudden wild longing for the feel of his arms around her, and the fierce, ravishing touch of his mouth on hers, and something of the depth of her feelings must have drawn his eyes to her, for she found herself looking directly into them for a brief second. It startled her so much that she coloured furiously and hastily lowered her eyes to the hands on her lap, her heart thudding hard and fast.

'You admire Dimitri?'

The question jolted her back to reality and she stared blankly at Madame Karamalis for a moment before she gathered her wits, choosing her words with care. 'He's a very considerate employer, *madame*, and I enjoy working for him.'

'And do you also enjoy being kissed by him?' Stunned for a moment, Carey stared at her, but before she had done more than shake her head, the old lady pressed a hand over hers and smiled faintly. 'Do not look so alarmed, *pethí*,' she told her kindly. 'I know my son, and I have already said that you are a very attractive young woman. If I embarrass you I will say no more.'

Carey had never felt so horribly exposed and vulnerable in her life. For kindly though Madame Karamalis was, the very fact of her remarking that she knew her son and therefore had guessed he had kissed her, made her feel as she did. Like just one more woman in his no doubt crowded love life.

She had already noticed that Niki was no longer in sight and she used any excuse to make her escape from those kindly but knowing eyes. Maybe the remark had been meant as a warning; maybe not, but she was too sensitive where Dimitri was concerned, and the noise and gaiety of the wedding was suddenly overwhelming.

Getting up from her chair, she smoothed down her dress, sounding as matter-of-fact as possible in the circumstances. 'I haven't seen Niki for some time,' she said, 'I think I'll go and see where he's got to, if you'll excuse me, *madame*.'

'He will not be far away,' Madame Karamalis assured her, and the fact that she seemed to know exactly why she was going did nothing at all to help. 'There are many other children for him to play with, Thespinís Gordon, you need not concern yourself.'

Carey gave a shaky little laugh, recalling another occasion when Niki had taken advantage of her distraction to wander off alone. 'Oh, I know Niki,' she said, 'and there's no guarantee that he hasn't gone off alone somewhere and is into mischief. He's a bit too adventurous sometimes.'

'Just as my son Dimitri was,' Madame Karamalis observed softly, and shook her head. 'Do not limit him too much, *pethí*, it is good that he grows like Dimitri.'

'But Dimitri will be quick to blame me if he gets into trouble,' Carey insisted, pulling a wry face. 'Please excuse me, *madame*, while I go and reassure myself.'

The old lady merely inclined her head, but there was a deep, thoughtful look in the fading dark eyes as they watched her, that Carey would rather not have noticed. It was irresistible as she made her way among the crowded tables to take one more look in Dimitri's direction, and as she did so Carey realised that he had already missed her. He was looking at the place where she had been sitting and frowning, and her heart beat with wild urgency. Suppose he should follow her——

She found Niki playing with a crowd of other children and he was quite content to stay there so that she had no qualms about leaving him, especially in view of Madame Karamalis's expressed opinion. Instead of returning to the old lady, however, she took a stroll among the trees and shrubs, along a quiet path she found, where the tumult of the party was barely audible, and eventually sat down on a seat that was almost completely overgrown by a huge oleander.

It was so much less disquieting sitting there than watching Dimitri; so aggressively masculine as he danced the ancient dances of Greece; powerful and virile and infinitely disturbing. Swiftly on the alert suddenly when she heard voices, she instantly recognised the woman's voice as Minerva Thoulou, and it was entirely instinct that made her lean forward slightly so that she could see through the thinner branches of the oleander, for she had never heard Minerva laugh before.

It was a low, husky and definitely sexy laugh, and Carey felt a brief qualm of conscience as she looked at her, for they could have no idea she was close by, and the situation was not one that should have an onlooker, she realised. Minerva was with a man barely as tall as herself, and stockily built, hatless and dark-haired, and although there was something vaguely familar about him, Carey couldn't actually recognise him.

She was about to show herself when once again that low laughter shivered in the stillness and Minerva swept off the hat she wore, shaking out her hair in a gesture so abandoned it startled Carey. Her usually grave face was bright and animated and her black eyes sparkled as she tipped her head, and another thrill of laughter was silenced almost at once when the man pulled her into his arms and kissed her.

Escape seemed even less easy now, and Carey sat there, well back in her seat so that she could no longer see them, wondering how she was going to slip away without being seen. She had completely forgotten about the tiny posy of flowers that she was carrying, one of many thrown into the crowd of guests by the bride, and as she shifted uneasily it rolled off her lap and into the middle of the path in full view.

The silence that followed was almost tangible, and Carey could feel her heart pounding anxiously as she waited. There was a soft, urgent flurry of Greek, followed by the sound of retreating feet, and she was on the point of sighing her relief when Minerva Thoulou appeared in front of her suddenly.

A pink flush still warmed her thin cheeks, and her normally firm mouth had a soft look, as if the touch of that passionate kiss still lingered there. There was neither accusation nor embarrassment on the curiously still features, only a kind of wariness, and Carey did not know what to say or do. 'Thespinís Gordon.' It was only when she hesitated to go on that Carey realised she didn't know what to say, and felt pity for her.

For someone like Minerva to be caught in a situation such as she had just witnessed must be more of an ordeal than for most people, and Carey was almost convinced she had discovered something that the rest of the Karamalis family knew nothing about. Everything seemed to point that way; the seemingly secret meeting, Minerva's wariness and the fact that the man had quickly disappeared.

'I came looking for somewhere cool to sit for a few minutes,' Carey explained hesitantly. 'I didn't expect to see anyone else.'

Minerva stood looking down at the tiny bunch of flowers at her feet for a moment, then she bent and picked it up, holding it to her nose for a moment before handing it back. 'You have been here for long?'

'Not very long, Kyria Thoulou, only a few minutes, that's all.'

Minerva's black eyes had the brilliance of jet and were more animated than Carey had ever seen them, and it occurred to her that Minerva, for all her gauntness, had something of the same beauty that Aliki had had. 'You saw?' she asked, and Carey saw no other way but to admit it.

'I didn't mean to, Kyria Thoulou, and when I realised, I sat back and kept out of sight. I wanted to leave, but it wasn't easy without you seeing me.'

'You will tell?'

She was anxious, and Carey looked at her with a hint of reproach. 'No, of course I won't tell, Kyria Thoulou; what you do is your own affair.'

'They would not—understand,' Minerva explained, and there was such anxiety both in her voice and her eyes that Carey's heart went out to her. Did the Karamalis ever understand their women? she wondered. 'You liked Aliki?'

Taken by surprise for a moment, Carey eventually nodded. 'Yes, I liked her very much, in fact. She was so vitally alive it was hard to believe when she died.'

'You thought us too—harsh, perhaps?'

It wasn't an easy question to answer in the circumstances, and because it was Minerva Carey hesitated about how honest to be. 'I don't know just what your attitudes are to certain situations,' she said cautiously. 'I feel that on the whole people should be able to do as they like with their own lives, although of course it does make a difference when there's a child involved.'

'You believe that Aliki—anyone, should lead life as they choose?' The nod Carey gave was slight and rather hesitant, but Minerva seemed not to notice it. 'She was happy?'

Her avid interest in her sister's affair must have some significance, Carey felt, and wondered if Minerva now found herself in a similar position. On that account she served up a half-truth because she lacked the courage to be too honest. 'Most of the time I think she was happy,' she said, but Minerva was obviously not interested in reservations.

'Ah!' Obviously it was what she wanted to hear, and her bright dark eyes gleamed with an unfamiliar warmth, her chin angled in a way that made her appear more truly Karamalis than she ever had before. 'That is what I wished to know—*efharisto*, Thespinís Gordon, *efharisto*!'

What exactly she was being thanked for so warmly, Carey wasn't sure, unless it was for relieving Minerva's conscience after all these years. It was by mutual consent that they turned and walked together along the path through the shrubbery, back towards the wedding feast, and Carey took one or two curious sidelong glances at her companion as they walked.

Minerva was the last person she would have imagined having a secret lover, and she was still convinced that no one in the family knew about him; those anxious questions about her intentions proved that. But she recalled how often Minerva had gone out in her car lately, and as they approached a division in the path she recalled a remark of Niki's, when he had been asking about Dimitri's kiss bringing her back to life. 'I think Thía Minerva got saved,' he had remarked, and neither she nor Dimitri had noticed at the time. Minerva was obviously very capable of keeping her own counsel, and only chance had given her away; on two occasions, presumably.

Whether or not she was going in search of her man-friend again, Carey had no idea, but at the division of the path Minerva took the longer way round to the front of the house. Touching her arm lightly, she smiled at Carey, her eyes only slightly evasive; perhaps a little shy. 'I am most grateful to you, Thespinís Gordon,' she whispered, as if even on the edge of that noisy, joyful crowd she feared being overheard. '*Efharisto* and—*hérete*!'

Watching her tall and almost regal figure walking

away from her, Carey frowned a little uneasily, for she had the strangest feeling that she had either said or done something that she was going to regret. Although at the moment she couldn't imagine what it might be.

CHAPTER SEVEN

CAREY did not bother to hurry the following morning because she thought it unlikely that anyone would be around after the wedding festivities. The reception had gone on until well into the night, and Niki had eventually fallen asleep on her lap; he was still sleeping when she looked in on him as usual in the morning, so she decided to leave him and went down to breakfast alone.

She had been almost right about no one being around, for when she appeared Dimitri had the breakfast table to himself, and she pulled a face as she walked along to join him. Dimitri, of course, would make it business as usual, no matter how hectic the night before had been, but whether or not anyone else had followed his example she didn't know, and she smiled at him enquiringly as she took the seat opposite to him.

'Am I first or last?' she asked, and he replied without looking up from some official-looking papers he was looking through.

'Neither,' he said enigmatically, and she frowned.

There was something about him this morning that rang warning bells and she wondered what had happened to cause it. 'No, of course,' she said. 'You were first and you're still here.'

He said nothing for a moment, yet she had the feeling that he was very much aware of her and on the verge of saying something. Then he looked up suddenly and directly at her, his black eyes deep and shadowed. 'Did you enjoy the wedding?'

Carey paused to smile at the young manservant who
brought her rolls and coffee. 'Very much, thank you,' she
said as the man departed. 'Although I'm still feeling a bit
woolly-headed after all the wine I drank; I'm not an hab-
itual drinker and it goes to my head.'

She studied him while he was preoccupied with his
papers, and yet again tried to fathom the reason for that
indefinable air about him. A cream shirt flattered his dark
skin and she took note of the fact that the pulse in his
throat was beating hard and fast, confirming her suspicion
that something was bothering him. There was further confirmation in the tight set of his mouth too, and a slight line
between his brows. Nor did she believe his attention was
as firmly fixed on the papers he was studying as it appeared
to be.

'I noticed that you did not stay with the dancers for
very long,' he said, still without looking up, 'and you
looked very flushed. I didn't realise the cause was too
much wine.'

Carey bit back the retort on the tip of her tongue and
took a fortifying sip of coffee first. She had been more
under the influence of the local wine than she realised, but
not nearly as much as most of the other guests, and certainly not as much as Dimitri was implying. 'I was very
hot and I simply couldn't keep up the pace; it wasn't
because I was too pie-eyed to stand up!' she told him, and
very deliberately used the vernacular, feeling a faint tri-
umph when he looked up and frowned. 'I mean that because I was flushed and laughing and couldn't manage to
keep up with your energetic countrymen, it doesn't mean
I was too drunk to stay on my feet! I should never have
attempted it in the first place.'

'Yet you joined in willingly enough,' Dimitri suggested,
and Carey raised her brows, looking at him over the rim
of her cup.

'I was roped in without being given much chance to

refuse,' she informed him pertly. 'I didn't think it was wise to argue with my employer!'

He frowned, but let it pass for the moment, obviously because he had something else on his mind. 'And having left the dance, you then disappeared.'

Where it was leading, Carey had no idea, but she was certain that he was taking a definite direction and she watched him curiously when his attention was again given to the papers by his plate. 'I didn't disappear either,' she argued. 'I went to check on Niki first and then went to find somewhere cooler for a while; it was too hot being in that crowd and I'm still not used to your climate. I did notice you frowning at my empty seat just after I left,' she added with a touch of bravado, 'but it didn't occur to me that I should have asked for permission before I went for a walk to cool off.'

'Damn you, Carey!' His sudden violence stunned her, but it was gone as quickly as it had come, and he was again sifting through those wretched papers; something that was beginning to irritate her to the extent that she had to keep a firm grip on herself. 'If you did not disappear,' he went on, 'then I cannot imagine where you were only a few minutes later, for I could find no sign of you on the path I took.'

So he *had* come after her! Carey's heart began a wild urgent beat as she remembered her quick dismissal of the possibility, and she stared at him for a moment trying to guess what his motive had been in following her, and regretting the fact that she had met Minerva in the quiet secrecy of the shrubbery instead.

'Maybe—maybe I went in a different direction,' she ventured in a rather small voice, and to her chagrin he merely shrugged.

Madame Karamalis had seemed to take his having kissed her as only what was to be expected, and Dimitri himself appeared to take it all just as casually. She never would understand them, she told herself despairingly, and she was thankful that she had only another two weeks with them, or she could well be sorry.

Then she noticed he was neatly stacking the papers into a pile before laying them down on the table again, and he leaned back in his chair with his hands curved over the edge of the table, fixing her with that infinitely disturbing black gaze. 'Did you arrange to meet my sister, Carey, or was it by accident?'

Startled, Carey stared at him, and her heart was thudding harder than ever when she took note of that hard-set mouth. 'You mean Kyria Thoulou?' she asked.

'I have only one sister, Carey, as you well know!'

This, she thought dazedly as she tried to gather her wits, was what he had been leading up to ever since she came and joined him. Somehow he must have learned about Minerva's man-friend, and her worry was that Minerva might think she had given her away. She wouldn't like that to happen because she liked Minerva.

'I know you saw her and talked to her,' he went on, 'and when you've finished your breakfast I would like to talk to you about it.'

'I met her by accident,' Carey insisted, too shaken now to go on with her breakfast, 'and we didn't talk about anything that would be of interest to anyone else.' That wasn't true and Dimitri knew it, she could see from his eyes. 'We were only together for a few minutes, that's all.'

'I would like to hear what you said,' Dimitri insisted, and gathered up the papers again. It wasn't anger, she realised, that made him so tense, but some equally passionate emotion that burned deep and made it hard for him to maintain that air of restraint that had only briefly given way. Standing facing her, he looked down, dark and brooding as a figure of vengeance, so that she shivered inwardly and dropped her eyes. 'When you have eaten breakfast, come and find me in the small *salon*,' he told her. 'I shall wait for you.'

Her heart was beating so hard that it almost choked

her, but she did manage to remember that Niki was still in bed, and she had to attend to him very soon. 'I left Niki asleep,' she began, but he interrupted her brusquely.

'Katina will attend to him. Come to the small *salon* as soon as you have finished breakfast.'

He was gone before she could say another word, and as she watched him go striding off along the path through the shrubbery, Carey wondered if Minerva had already been interrogated, or if her turn was yet to come. In fact she had no more appetite for breakfast, but she did take a few minutes to think about her position where Minerva was concerned. She couldn't see that a woman of thirty and a widow could be scolded like a naughty child, so what good Dimitri thought could be served by asking her, Carey, questions about it she didn't see.

She never knew what impulse took her to the *salon* before she went in search of Dimitri, but there was some hope lurking in the back of her mind that Minerva might be there and she could assure her of her silence. When she opened the door the room was quiet, too quiet, and every eye turned on her at once, though no one even murmured the conventional '*kalimera*' but just looked at her.

Andoni and Rhoda sat together in one corner of the room with Damon nearby, and Madame Karamalis occupied her usual chair, her eyes suggesting that she had been crying recently. But it was the absence of Minerva that troubled Carey most, and as she closed the door behind her, she anxiously moistened her lips, glancing across at the small *salon* where Dimitri did work at home on occasion.

He probably heard her coming, for high heels made an unmistakable clicking sound on the tiled hall floor, and she had scarcely time to tap on the door before she was brusquely told to go in. Her legs felt horribly unsteady, in fact her whole body was trembling and she despaired of her own weakness where Dimitri was concerned.

When she walked in he was standing by the window, a

familiar stance that recalled another occasion, and she had a moment to take brief stock of him again. He stood with a hand either side of the window frame, a stance that pulled his shirt tautly across a broad back, and the strong muscular arms that supported him made her shiver at the remembered thrill of their strength. She recalled the gentleness of those big hands too, and her colour was high when he turned and looked at her, her grey eyes bright and wary.

Steady-eyed, he regarded her in silence for a moment, and try as she would, Carey could not subdue the wild notions that filled her head and had nothing at all to do with Minerva and her lover. 'Did you finish breakfast?' he asked, and the very ordinariness of the question startled her.

'As much as I wanted, thank you.'

'Hmm.' He indicated a chair on her side of a small table, sometimes used as a desk. 'Sit down, Carey.'

It was almost automatic to do as he said, but she shook her head at the last minute, deterred by the prospect of having him tower over her. 'I—I'd rather stand until I know what this is all about,' she told him, and Dimitri frowned.

'You choose to act as if I am accusing you,' he said, and came across the room, standing immediately in front of her and watching her with eyes that burned darkly between their thick lashes and were curiously affecting. 'Please sit down,' he insisted. 'You disturb me too much while you stand there with your hands folded so virtuously in front of you!'

Carey coloured furiously, but she unclasped the offending hands and placed them on the edge of the table behind her instead. 'I know you're going to accuse me of something,' she said. 'You're treating me as if I've done something criminal, and I can't for the life of me think what I've done to deserve it.'

He was making a supreme effort, Carey recognised,

when he heaved his shoulders in resignation, and she
supposed he made some kind of apology. 'If I have misjudged you I will apologise,' he promised. 'This is an unhappy business and I only wish I could be convinced that
you had nothing whatever to do with it. Unfortunately
everything points to you being involved, and I must know
how deeply—for my own peace of mind.'

'Your—your peace of mind?'

Anger she could have understood, but this strange mood
of concern was disturbing, and Carey realised just how
hard it was going to be keeping Minerva's secret if he
questioned her outright. Dimitri was much too hard to
resist.

'You have already said that you spoke with Minerva
yesterday,' he said. 'I am asking you to say what you
spoke about to her, Carey, and when.'

There was such a look in his eyes that she moistened her
lips again anxiously. 'It wasn't long after you saw me
leave the party.' She stopped there, knowing she ought
not to go on if she was to keep her promise to Minerva,
and she shook her head slowly. 'I can't tell you what was
said because—because I promised not to say a word. I
promised Minerva that I'd keep it to myself and I can't
let her down.' She looked up for a moment, wary and
appealing at the same time. 'You know something about
it,' she added in a small voice, 'or you wouldn't be trying
to make me tell you what I know.'

She had expected him to lose his temper when she flatly
refused to answer, but instead he gave a great sigh of
resignation and turned his back once more, to go and
stand by the window. He stood there for several minutes
with his hands on the frame again and his head bowed
slightly, so that for some reason she felt pity for him,
something she had never imagined was possible, and her
reaction was completely instinctive.

'Dimitri, I'm sorry!'

He turned from the window, and with the light behind

him his face was thrown into shadow, so that every deep, chiselled line of his features seemed deeper and darker, and his eyes black and unfathomable. 'Then tell me how much you said to her,' he said, and his voice was quieter now and more persuasive.

She couldn't not answer him, Carey knew; it was her weakness that she couldn't refuse him, but when she did she would be half-way to giving away Minerva's secret. 'We—talked about Aliki,' she ventured, and he put a hand to his forehead as if that was the very last thing he wanted to hear.

'And you told her that Aliki was happy with her lover?'

Carey's head was spinning, for unless Minerva herself had told him that, she didn't see how he could know. Yet if Minerva had told him he would have no need to question her, and she recalled uneasily Minerva's absence from the family group in the *salon*. 'I may have done,' she agreed, but shook her head agitatedly. 'Why don't you ask Minerva about this, she could——'

'I cannot do that!' Something in his voice, some dull note of finality, sent a shiver running through her and she looked up at him anxiously. Her heart was thudding violently hard and making it difficult for her to think clearly. Dimitri ran a hand through the thick hair at the back of his head and she thought she had never seen such despair in his eyes before. 'Minerva did not come home last night—she has run away with her lover!'

'Oh no!'

A hand over her mouth, Carey stared at him. She had been right to suspect the family knew nothing about him at all, and she understood now why Dimitri wanted to know what had passed between her and Minerva, although heaven knew how he knew they had seen one another. That was a mystery that still remained to be solved.

She didn't want to believe that her little speech about Aliki having the right to choose her own way of life had

had any effect, but in her heart Carey knew it had. She had also allowed that Aliki was happy with her unconventional way of life, and Minerva had obviously taken her sister's experience as her guide, and Carey's assurance as encouragement enough to follow her example.

'In the name of heaven,' Dimitri demanded, 'why did *you* have to become involved?'

There seemed little point in hiding anything from him now, for discretion could serve no purpose, and she shook her head slowly. 'I had no intention of being involved,' she said in a small unhappy voice. 'I just happened to see them together for a few seconds when they didn't realise I was there, and I was trying to think of some way I could go without them seeing me. Then a posy I had on my lap rolled on to the path and Minerva saw it.'

'And the man with her?'

Carey recalled those retreating footsteps and shrugged uneasily. 'I think Minerva must have sent him away. I couldn't understand what she said, but she sounded very insistent, and then I heard someone walking away.' Feeling that he still saw her as in some way to blame, she looked up at him anxiously. 'I had no idea what she meant to do,' she insisted huskily.

Dimitri said nothing for a moment, then he took a letter from his shirt pocket and unfolded it while Carey watched him curiously. Translating as he went along, he read part of it out to her in his neat, pedantic English.

'*I have been told that Aliki was happy even though we condemned her for doing what she did, and I will be as happy as she was, although I know that you will condemn me too. It was also said that Aliki—that everyone of us has the right to lead life as we choose, and I am convinced this is right. No one is to blame for my decision, but I now have the courage to take this step and know that I can be as happy as Aliki was*'.

He broke off and stood for a moment looking at her with an expression in his eyes that she found hard to face. 'Dimitri, please believe me, I only talked to her for a few minutes.'

'But you told her these things,' he insisted. 'No one else knew enough about Aliki's life at that time to have told Minerva how happy she was.'

It was true and she couldn't deny it, but she would have given anything to be able to. 'She asked about Aliki and I told her what I could without—making the situation sound too attractive, but please believe me, I hadn't any idea she'd do something like this. If I'd had any idea where it was leading I wouldn't have said a word about Aliki.' He was folding the letter again and putting it back into his pocket and she watched him anxiously. 'This man—is married too?'

'No, he is not married.'

'He's—someone you know?'

Dimitri was looking at her curiously, his eyes slightly narrowed. 'Did you not see him?' he asked, and she shook her head. 'You did not recognise him?'

That very vague moment of recognition did not count, she decided. 'No, should I have done?'

He looked for a moment as if he was in two minds whether or not to believe her. 'Minerva has eloped with her chauffeur, Carey.'

So that was it. There was nothing wrong with Minerva's choice, except in the eyes of her autocratic family. 'And that's why you're so—so shocked?' she asked. 'If the man isn't already married and Minerva loves him, I don't see why she shouldn't run away with him, even if he is *only* her chauffeur! I hope they'll be very happy together!'

'*Amín*,' Dimitri said softly, but there was something about the way he was looking at her that made her strangely uneasy, and somehow Carey knew she was about to be put firmly in her place. Not a new experience, but always a chastening one when Dimitri was involved. 'So, you are assuming that the fact of his being her chauffeur is what concerns us,' he said. 'Not for the first time you are misjudging us, Carey.'

Horribly afraid that he was about to prove it, Carey looked uneasy. 'If I am I'm sorry.'

'What is so—disturbing,' Dimitri went on in the same quiet voice, 'is the lack of understanding in one who should know us better than you do. Both my sisters have now made secret liaisons and neither has given a thought to the distress they have caused their mother. You cannot be expected to understand, Carey, but Greek families treasure their daughters, and their marriages are joyous occasions; think of Despina yesterday. It was like that with Minerva when she married. We grieved for her when Konstandi Thoulou was killed, do you not think we would have rejoiced to see her happy again?'

Carey nodded. 'Yes. Yes, I know you would.'

'Whoever the man was, if he was free to marry her, he would have been welcome if he made Minerva happy. Panos Petrakis is a free and honest man, whatever his position, and Minerva had no reason to suppose we would try to spoil her happiness. It is her lack of understanding of us—her family—that troubles us, not her choice of man.'

'Poor Minerva,' Carey said softly, 'she isn't like the rest of you, is she?'

'The rest of us!' Dimitri echoed, and she gasped when a hand slid under her chin and jerked her head upward with a hint of ruthlessness that set her heart racing. His eyes gleamed darkly and were much too close for comfort. 'You think us too proud?' he demanded. 'Too harsh in our judgments, hah?'

Carey met his eyes for a moment, her colour high and a glint of defiance in her eyes. 'You *are* proud!' she declared. 'And I can understand Minerva being too nervous to tell you about her man-friend; she probably *did* think you'd condemn her as you did Aliki!'

'The pride of Greece condemned Aliki,' Dimitri told her firmly. 'We treasure our women, and Aliki took a deliberate step against all we believe in.'

Carey sighed, as if she found it all too much to take in.

'She was as proud as any of the Karamalises,' she said, and when he laughed suddenly she stared at him, for it was the first time she had ever known him laugh.

His fingers on her jaw held her firmly but at the same time moved their tips in a light and infinitely disturbing caress, and his eyes gleamed at her like jet. 'You believe us so autocratic that we think only of our family pride, eh? What do you know of us, Carey? We have wealth, much more than most people, and from my mother we have breeding, but the Karamalis blood? My father was descended from one of the most villainous corsairs ever to plague the Mediterranean trade routes! He took his bride from one of his captives and he was a brutal and unfaithful husband, but he left six sons to carry on his name. The Karamalis pride is in our strength and our virility, not in any high-blooded lineage, Carey!'

She was trembling, affected as she always was by him, and he stood for a moment looking down into her eyes. Then both hands curved about her cheeks, cupping her face in his palms while he looked down at her mouth in a way that sent ripples of ice along her spine. Dimitri could arouse responses in her that no other man ever had, and no matter how she sought to control it, there was always that feeling of abandon to contend with whenever she was near him.

'I called you in to talk about Minerva,' he said, in a soft deep voice that suggested he had already lost sight of his original intention once, and was likely to do so again.

With her own heart thudding wildly in her breast, Carey had a brief mental picture of Minerva pulling off her hat, and of that reckless, abandoned laughter just a second before she was kissed. 'If you'd seen her face in those few moments before they knew I was there,' she murmured. 'She was—she was almost beautiful, like Aliki.'

'Like a woman in love,' Dimitri observed, and there was a sardonic glint in his eyes as he looked at her. 'Selfish too; like a woman in love she thought of nothing but her own happiness.'

'And why not?' she challenged, before he pressed his thumbs over her lips.

'Why not?' he echoed softly.

The deep blackness of his eyes came close, and for a moment Carey felt herself almost drowning in them. Then he touched her mouth with his pursed lips, brushing them lightly back and fourth until she gave a sigh and parted her lips, lifting her face eagerly, unresisting because she knew it was inevitable.

His hands were pressing her close, hard and firm on her back, and the arching softness of her body was fired with the fierce virility he had boasted of. Forcing her closer, until she had no strength of her own and reached up her arms to encircle his neck. Plunging downward, his mouth buried itself deep in hers, and there was suddenly nothing in the world but Dimitri, the possessive fierceness of his mouth, and her own exultant ecstasy.

Nothing, that is, until a voice somewhere intruded into the dream and snatched her back to the edge of reality. And she noticed that Dimitri's head was half turned, as if he expected someone to come into the room. Yet he didn't release her, but rested his hands just under her arms with the broad warmth of his palms firm on her breasts, and the press of his body still close enough to stir her senses.

Then high heels clicked busily on the hall floor, and a second after that Rhoda's voice shrilled angrily and broke the spell completely. Dimitri turned back to her, still holding her with hands that stroked lightly through the thin material of her dress. He shook his head slowly, and slid his hands upward to enclose her flushed cheeks, speaking so softly that his voice was a caress in itself.

'There is nothing to be done until Minerva chooses to come back to us,' he said, and just briefly that hurt look showed again in his eyes. 'We cannot make her return, only hope that she sees us more clearly standing off a little than she did close to.'

'She will,' Carey whispered, and he smiled faintly, bending to touch her mouth again with his.

'Go and wake Nikolas if he is not already awake,' he told her, 'while I do my best to convince Mamá that you are in no way to blame for what Minerva did.'

It was incredibly satisfying and comforting to have him ready to speak up for her, and she looked up at him with soft grey eyes. 'You will?'

'I will,' Dimitri confirmed quietly.

In some curious way he seemed to have already gone farther away from her, and when he took his hands from her cheeks it left her feeling oddly bereft. How quickly and easily he slipped back to normality after those moments of passion that left her emotionally shattered, and just for a moment as she looked at him, she almost hated him for his detachment.

'Dimitri——'

A swiftly arched brow quizzed her so that she caught her bottom lip hard between her teeth because she didn't know what to say to him, only that she didn't want him to go. It was a silence that expected something to happen and when nothing did he bent his head and kissed her mouth, speaking with his lips against hers.

'Go and get Nikolas from his bed,' he said. 'Quickly, brefoz mou!'

'I'm going!'

She turned, still not completely down to earth, and went hurrying across the room, and as she crossed the hall, she was still trying rather dazedly to decide how it was that no matter how angrily he started out, Dimitri so often seemed to end up kissing her. In view of Madame Karamalis's implication that it was a perfectly acceptable thing for him to do, and Dimitri's own careless attitude, Carey would undoubtedly be wise not to let it happen again. Maybe in the circumstances she should be glad that the month's notice he had demanded was already half completed.

When Niki was at school there was really very little for Carey to do, and she was stretched out on a sun-lounger beside the pool, feeling pleasantly lazy and relaxed. It was only very reluctantly that she opened her eyes when someone called out her name, and particularly when she recognised the voice.

'Carey! Ah, you are not asleep—that is good! *Kalimera!*'

She could feel the intensity of his gaze as he took in every detail of her figure, and the colour rose in her cheeks briefly, although she pretended not to notice his interest. 'Good morning, Mitso; how are you?' She would probably have been wiser to sit up, she realised, but she didn't want to encourage him to stay.

An over-indulgence of some sweet-smelling after-shave made her wrinkle her nose as Mitso placed a hand on each arm of her chair and leaned over her so that his face was only a foot or so above hers. The nearness of him actually warmed her skin like a physical touch, and from the way his eyes gleamed he knew exactly the effect he was having, showing his excellent teeth in a smile that was not entirely without malice. It was the first time Carey had seen him since he married Despina, and from the look of him marriage had done little, if anything, to change him.

'You do not look very pleased to see me,' he accused, and rather than tell him an outright lie by denying it, Carey took another course.

'How's Despina?' she asked, and just for a second that confident smile wavered slightly.

'Happy, of course,' he said, unconscious of any conceit. 'And you?'

Mitso shrugged. 'As always.' Carey was wearing a swimsuit; a new one she had bought recently because Niki insisted that she should learn to swim too, and Mitso's eyes moved slowly down the length of her slim shape, lingering appreciatively on the deep, plunging vee in the front. 'I can still appreciate the beautiful things in life, marriage does not blunt the senses.' His eyes again deliberately lingered. 'Nor the appetite.'

Made more than ever conscious of the revealing cut of the costume, Carey shifted uneasily. 'If you'll move out of my way,' she said, 'I'd like to sit up, Mitso.'

Instead of moving, however, he perched himself on the side of the chair and leaned even farther down so that his body pressed lightly on hers and his face hovered, taunting her with his eyes when he saw the colour that flooded into her face. 'Do not sit up on my account,' he murmured. 'I like you the way you are, my lovely; you cannot get away from me while you are lying on your back. I cannot remember a time when you did not try to get away from me, Carey, you have never been very nice to me.'

His mood troubled her, but there was no chance of her stamping the heel of her shoe on his foot this time and getting away. She either had to stay where she was or sit up and find herself in his arms. 'I won't try to get away if you'll just let me sit up,' she told him. 'You can't expect me to say I'm glad to see you when you start annoying me the moment you get here. Please, Mitso!'

His laughter trickled like ice along her spine and she could feel the too-rapid beat of her heart. There were times when Mitso alarmed her, for he was so different from Dimitri and she was never quite sure how to deal with him. He could be charming when he chose, but even his charm had a hint of malice, and she realised at last why it was she had always been so wary of him.

With a forefinger he traced a line down from her jaw to the softness of her neck and from there to the curve of her shoulder, then he put both hands on her shoulders suddenly, pinning her firmly to the cushions of the lounger. 'Now what will you do?' he teased, and Carey kept a firm hold on her rising temper.

'Scream for help, if necessary,' she told him, breathless

but adamant, and when he laughed again she looked at
him steadily. 'Don't think I won't, Mitso. You're a
married man, and I don't play around with other women's
husbands; whatever your opinion of English morals, that
isn't my scene!'

'Hah!' He sat back, but his eyes were black and gleaming and there was a touch of sulkiness about his mouth.
Married or not, it seemed to make little difference to his
determined pursuit of her, and she remembered how
Dimitri had warned her that he wouldn't give up until she
yielded. 'You are what is called a—a prude, no?' Carey
didn't answer him, but while he was at least temporarily
out of the way she managed to sit upright and reached
round for the jacket hanging on the back of her chair.
'You have two morals, I think,' Mitso went on. 'You lived
with Aliki when she was with her lover, and yet you
behave as if you know nothing about love.'

'For heaven's sake, Mitso,' she declared shortly, 'what
you have in mind has nothing at all to do with *love*!'

'Now you are the expert, eh?' His dark eyes challenged
her, and there was resentment in every word he spoke.
'You encouraged Minerva to run away with her lover,
though. Because it was *love*! Oh, I have heard from Rhoda
that you gave her advice and told her that she should do
as she wished with her life!'

'That isn't true!' With the jacket held close to her throat,
Carey looked at him and frowned. 'Dimitri accused me of
much the same thing until I explained what really
happened.'

'Ah, and he believed you, of course!' He curled his lip
derisively. 'We shall soon be scattered far and wide, but
you will never leave, will you, Carey?'

'I *am* leaving, in about two weeks' time, you know that.'
She looked at him uneasily. 'And what do you mean—
scattered far and wide?'

Mitso shrugged, his dark eyes watching her closely,
gleamingly bright as he leaned farther back on the lounger

and made it even harder for her to get up. 'Is it not so?' he demanded. 'Aliki is gone, I am gone and now Minerva. Soon it will be Andoni and Rhoda's turn and there will be no one to trouble you. Would Dimitri change his mind about Andoni if he thought you were leaving—really leaving? I think not!'

Carey was staring at him, unable to believe he was telling the truth, and she shook her head slowly. 'Dimitri knows I shall go the minute I've served my notice,' she insisted. 'Whatever he's changed his mind about it has nothing to do with me.'

Mitso shrugged his eloquent shoulders, and mockery showed in his eyes as he regarded her for a moment in silence. 'It is amusing in one way,' he said, 'that the one of us you like least has most reason to be grateful to you. Not that Rhoda *will* be grateful to you, because she will resent the reason behind the change. She will not like to think that Dimitri is getting rid of her because she slapped you.'

She couldn't believe it, of course, but somewhere deep in her heart a flutter of hope lurked that he *would* do something wildly uncharacteristic like that, and she briefly moistened her lips with the tip of her tongue. 'I—I don't see Dimitri getting rid of his sister-in-law, as you put it, on my account,' she told him. 'How could he—get rid of her?'

'By giving Andoni the London office,' Mitso said, and watched her with a glimmer of malice in his eyes. 'Had he not told you about it, Carey?'

'I doubt if he ever will,' she retorted swiftly, 'because it's absolute nonsense! You're making mischief, Mitso!'

'As you did when you told Dimitri about Rhoda going to London!'

Looking at him, Carey tried to find something of the charming young man who had fetched her and Niki from the airport, and caught just a glimpse of him for a moment. Mitso's rapid changes of mood were a characteristic he shared with Aliki and with Niki too, and she found them both confusing and intriguing.

'You are sorry?' he asked, and she looked at him curiously.

'For causing a family row? Yes, of course I am.'

'But not that she will not be sharing the same roof, surely?'

'I shan't be here to appreciate it,' Carey told him, 'but I am sorry that Madame Karamalis will be losing touch with one of her grandsons.'

Mitso shrugged carelessly. 'She will still have Aliki's brat to dote on.'

'Dimitri's son very soon now,' Carey corrected him quietly, and he showed his teeth in a gleaming satisfied smile.

'Adopted son,' he jeered. '*I* will have my own sons before very long!'

Of course he was bound to notice the colour that flooded into her face, and she wished desperately for some way of escape that wouldn't involve her clambering over him and leaving herself wide open to any move he might make while she did. Mitso was quite shrewd enough to know the reason for that warm flush right after mentioning Dimitri not having sons of his own.

'Or do you suppose Dimitri will one day father his own sons?' he asked, and the glow of mockery in his eyes taunted her unmercifully.

'I don't see why not.' Carey spoke quietly and with as much coolness as she could manage, but it was a subject she dared not discuss at any length without giving herself away. 'And I think this conversation's gone quite far enough, Mitso. Move over and let me get out, it's time I got dressed, it's nearly lunchtime.'

'Plenty of time yet.' He sat well back on the lounger, watching her with a faint and oddly disturbing smile on his lips. Then he shifted nearer suddenly and again put his hands on her shoulders, his fingers digging in hard. 'First——' he said, and pulled her towards him, his eyes glittering and a glint of determination in his eyes.

To take her into his arms, however, he was obliged to change his position slightly, and while he was distracted for the moment, Carey squirmed out of reach suddenly, and ducked, scrabbling helplessly on the shiny cushions for a moment before she got sufficient purchase to push herself free. She actually managed to get to her feet, but he grabbed her arm before she could get away and pulled hard. 'No, Mitso!'

He was laughing, confident of victory, but she tugged at her arm and, because he was slightly off balance, he was forced to let go again. She heard him cursing in his own tongue as she started to run along the tiled edge of the pool with the light jacket she wore over her swimsuit flying wide. Then he was on his feet too and coming after her.

Instinct alone dictated her actions, and without hesitation, as he closed on her, she veered to one side and jumped into the pool, hearing him curse again as he was left on the side with her jacket in his hands. Her first effort was to get to the surface as quickly as she could, for her swimming lessons had not progressed far enough yet for her to be very confident, and she was breathing hard when she eventually broke the surface and shook back the hair out of her eyes.

Her jacket was floating just a few feet away, where Mitso had obviously thrown it, and Mitso himself was striding angrily along the path back to the house. It was unfortunate that she had chosen to jump into the deep end, but she thought she might just about make the side if she took her time and thought about what she was doing. Ever since that near-fatal ducking in the sea she found herself much too inclined to panic, but she tried not to think about it as she laboriously swept each arm up and over in turn.

'Carey?' She looked up and once more threw the wet hair out of her eyes to find herself looking up into Dimitri's darkly anxious face. 'Are you O.K.?'

Somehow she managed to smile, and at the same moment as her hands touched the bar at the poolside his hands reached down to her. Strong brown fingers clasped tightly around her wrists, and he crouched there supporting her for a moment and looking down into her face. 'You were in the *salon*,' she guessed, and laughed as she paddled her legs and feet. 'One day Mitso will learn that whenever he misbehaves himself on that particular spot he can be seen from the *salon* window!'

'Will you tell him?'

'No!'

Dimitri said nothing, but he straightened up suddenly and gave a sharp tug that hauled her bodily out of the water in a shower of rainbow drops that splashed his slacks with little dark spots. He seemed not to mind that she stood close enough for her wet body to make him wet too, and he kept a hold on her wrists while he looked down into her face, flushed and glistening.

'You must have been desperate to escape him if you jumped into the pool like that,' he said, and his hands slipped instead under her arms, caressingly light on her skin.

'I—I was angry.' She looked up, blinking away the drops that clung to her lashes and still breathing through parted lips. 'I'm afraid marriage hasn't done a thing to reform your brother,' she went on in a light, shivery little voice. 'You did warn me that he wouldn't stop until I gave in.'

'And you told me you never would.'

'Nor will I!' She shivered slightly at the touch of his hands, and Dimitri gazed at her still with those deep, fathomless eyes of his. 'I took the only way out,' she went on, trying desperately to still the clamour of her senses at the nearness of him. 'I suppose it would have been more to the point if I'd pushed Mitso into the water to cool off!'

'This costume——' He looked down at the flimsy,

clinging wet swim suit and his hands slid down to her waist, broad palms and long fingers spread over the gentle curve of her hips. 'It would tempt any man with blood in his veins, *kopéla*, I cannot find it in my heart to blame him too much.'

Her heart was racing like a wild thing, and Carey knew just how tempted he was himself. But Dimitri wasn't like Mitso; she wouldn't run from Dimitri. Just a few steps and that view from the *salon* would be blocked by the spread of a huge oleander, and she found herself drawn into its shelter almost without realising it. Just briefly common sense raised its head and she remembered how matter-of-fact Madame Karamalis had been about his kissing her, and how untouched Dimitri himself seemed to emerge from those wild moments of passion. But still she could do nothing about her own response.

His arms slid around her, one hand pressed into the small of her back and bringing her close to the hard, fierce virility she remembered so well. And because her wetness had soaked into his shirt, when she lifted her arms and put them around his neck their bodies were so close, so bound together, it was as if they were both naked.

The hard thudding beat of her heart was like a drum, so violent that it almost deafened her, and she caught her breath suddenly when one hand slid around and rested for a moment on the pulsing curve of her breast. 'Your heart beats so hard,' he murmured against the muffling dampness of her hair. 'Is it still for fear of Mitso, or for fear of me, Carey?'

'Maybe a little of both,' Carey whispered, and turned her head slightly to brush her lips on the dark skin in the opening of his shirt.

His fingers grasped a handful of her hair and he held back her head while he looked down into her face with a faint, half-mocking smile. 'You fear me?' he demanded softly, as if he knew very well that it wasn't fear she felt. 'I do not believe it, *oreos mou*!'

He touched her lips with his, lightly at first, and then with that hard, demanding fierceness she could never forget. Every nerve in her body tingled with a desire she could do nothing to subdue, nor did she want to, no matter what common sense decreed. Pressing close, she yielded up her mouth and the soft coolness of her body to a passion that was like nothing she had known before, and those big, gentle hands stroked and persuaded her towards complete surrender.

The thudding beat of her own heart and the soft murmured words that breathed against her ear seemed part of a separate existence, and it was as if nothing mattered but the two of them in a small scented world that was bounded by the sheltering mass of the oleander. One hand slipped down to the front of his shirt and she found it wet, gazing at it curiously for a moment before she realised the cause.

'You're very wet,' she whispered huskily, and Dimitri looked at her with his eyes heavy-lidded and gleaming blackly.

'Much less so than you are,' he reminded her with a faint smile, and raised one arm slightly to consult the watch on his wrist. 'And if you are not to appear at lunch looking like a water nymph you will have to dry and get dressed, *mikros ena*.'

He brushed a hand over her damp hair, but still held her close with one arm, and he started just as jerkily as she did when the sound of a metal gong being beaten shattered the stillness of the garden, and sent the birds fluttering upwards in shrill protest. Her heart beating wildly, Carey looked up at him while her fingers dug hard into his arms, then she glanced briefly over her shoulder in the direction of the house where it seemed to have come from.

'What—what was that?' she whispered.

Dimitri seemed to have recovered remarkably quickly after that initial start, and she caught a faint hint of amusement in his eyes when she looked at him again.

Easing her away from him slightly, he nevertheless still kept his hands on her arms. 'I suspect it was Mitso,' he said, and Carey looked at him in startled disbelief.

'Mitso?'

'There is an old brass gong in the small *salon*,' Dimitri explained, 'and when Andoni and Rhoda were betrothed it was a favourite trick of his to wait until they were walking in the garden and then startle them by taking the gong to the open window and banging on it. Of course he was then no more than nine years old, but it seems his sense of timing has not deserted him!'

Flushing warmly, Carey drew back. She found that hint of amusement too discomfiting in the present situation and once again rued her own willingness to be enticed by Dimitri's skilful seduction. Mitso would have passed Dimitri on his way out when he went back to the house, and he would resent it as bitterly as he always did, that Dimitri was stepping into a situation where he had been rebuffed. Knowing that Dimitri was on his way out to her would be provocation enough for Mitso.

'How childish!'

She pulled herself free of him and quite instinctively clasped her arms with her hands, for she had never felt more exposed and vulnerable in her life before. Dimitri found it amusing, or so his manner suggested, while she felt as if something wonderful had been reduced to a light hearted incident to be laughed over by the two brothers.

She would have been happier if she could have had her jacket to cover her, but that was floating on the surface of the pool still, and her sandals were still alongside the lounger she had been using. She had only the skimpy protection of the dark blue swimsuit that clung to her like a second skin, and she had never been more conscious of her own body as she was when she turned swiftly away from him and half ran, back to the house, leaving a small pool at his feet where she had been standing.

'Carey!'

She ignored the call and ran for the privacy of her own room. One day, she vowed, she would learn not to be so easily persuaded, but in the meantime she couldn't find it in her heart to be thankful the day was rapidly approaching when she wouldn't need her powers of resistance.

CHAPTER EIGHT

IT was a very important day for Niki and at the moment he seemed rather overawed by the prospect. Not that he was any less enthusiastic about the adoption, but it was something completely outside his experience and he was, naturally enough, a little apprehensive about what was going to happen to him.

Carry herself felt a kind of sickening sensation as she took even greater pains with his appearance than usual, for Dimitri would expect him to be especially spick and span today of all days. In a smart blue gaberdine suit with a white shirt and a blue tie, he looked rather younger than his six years, and somehow touchingly vulnerable, so that she felt a lump in her throat for a moment.

So much seemed to be happening so quickly lately. First Mitso's wedding and all the attendant fuss and confusion over Minerva's elopement, and now Niki's adoption, only a few days later, and very soon now her own departure would cause another upheaval. In her life at least, though what effect it would have on others she couldn't guess.

Because she dreaded the task herself Carey kept hoping that Dimitri would help by breaking the news of her going to Niki, but so far he'd made no move in that direction or she would have known. Niki should have been told by now, she knew, but she found the task no easier than she had at the beginning, although now she had to admit it was for a slightly different reason.

Niki had become so closely involved with Dimitri that there was just the chance he wouldn't mind her going quite so much as he would once have done, and it was something she felt would be hard to take. Not only because it would mean Niki was less attached to her, but because he might in the circumstances not raise so many objections to her going as he had in the past. She had only recently faced the fact that while Niki had been her reason for coming there, it was becoming increasingly obvious that Dimitri had just as much to do with her wanting to remain.

Ever since that day by the pool she had taken pains to avoid being alone with him, but the fact remained that he attracted her in a way no one else ever had. Common sense told her that leaving was by far her best move, but her feelings for Dimitri had little to do with common sense; she could only think about strong arms and gentle hands, and a mouth that ravished her senses.

She was so preoccupied with her own situation that it was a moment or two before she realised how very quiet and subdued Niki was for him. Putting down the hairbrush, she looked at him enquiringly and smiled. 'O.K.?' she asked.

He nodded, but met her eyes for only a moment, then looked down at his feet instead, and there was a suggestion of a frown between his brows. 'Is it time?' he asked, and he looked so solemn and unsmiling that she took both his hands and smiled at him encouragingly.

'There's no reason to look so worried about it, darling,' she told him. 'All that happens is that you talk to one or two people for a moment or two and then Thíos—your *papá* signs some papers and it's all over. It's what you both want, isn't it?'

Niki nodded, but he was brushing a hand back and forth over his black curls in a way he always did whenever he was uncertain or troubled about something. 'Carey—Thía

Rhoda says I won't really be Thíos Dimitri's son even when he's 'dopted me. She said I'm Aliki's—I can't remember the name she called me, but Thíos Andoni was very cross and scolded her about it.'

It needed no great effort on Carey's part to guess what name Rhoda had called him, and for a moment she hated Andoni's spiteful wife with a ferocity that surprised her. Thank heaven she would soon be on her way to London and no longer around to make Niki's life a misery; for whatever precautions Dimitri took to prevent it, he couldn't always be around to protect him from Rhoda and Damon's spite. It was some consolation, she told herself, that Andoni had been angry.

Trying to reassure him, she smiled as she brushed the hair back from his forehead where it had already flopped from its tidy brushing. 'But of course you'll be your *papá*'s son,' she told him. 'You mustn't listen to Thía Rhoda, Niki. She's cross because she doesn't want your uncle to adopt you, that's all.'

'Why?' Niki asked, inevitably, and Carey realised what a rod she had made for her own back when she let slip that casual observation.

'Oh, it's a long story, darling,' she told him, 'and one you'll understand better when you're older. There's a great deal of money involved, and money always causes trouble, especially a lot of money. Because your uncle is adopting you, you'll get a share one day. But your new *papá* will tell you all about it one day when you're bigger.'

But Niki was frowning and when he frowned he looked quite alarmingly like Dimitri. 'You mean I shall get Thía Rhoda's share?' he asked. 'Is that why she doesn't want me to be 'dopted?'

'It simply means that there won't be quite so much to go around,' Carey told him, and brought the subject firmly to an end by consulting her wristwatch. 'And I think we'd better go, in case Thíos Dimi—your *papá* is waiting for you, don't you?' He nodded, still solemn-faced. 'And couldn't you manage a smile, Niki? This is your big day, remember?'

As always he responded quickly to encouragement and turned impulsively to hug her for a moment, heedless of possible damage to his smart suit. 'Yayá Karamalis is coming with us,' he said. 'I wish you were too, Carey.'

Carey wished she could too, but she didn't say so because she knew Niki well enough to guess that he would ask Dimitri to take her with them, and as she was so soon to leave them, she didn't really have any place in his new life. Instead she smiled and straightened his tie before taking his hand firmly in hers.

'You can tell me all about it when you come home,' she told him. 'Now I think we'd better go. All ready?'

Which was more or less what Dimitri asked him when he met them in the hall a few minutes later. But it seemed to Carey that Dimitri was giving more of his attention to her than to Niki, so that she began to wonder if he was going to suggest she went with them after all. 'What will you do this morning, Carey?' he asked. 'Have you anything special in mind?'

'Nothing very much.' She shrugged off any suggestion that her plans involved anything important in the hope of encouraging him. 'I thought I might go into Athens and do some shopping, that's all. I haven't anything special to get but just one or two things to—to take back.'

He ignored the reminder completely, and Niki appeared not to have noticed anything untoward. 'Good,' Dimitri said. 'Then I suggest you get Roussos to drive you in my mother's car and meet Nikolas and me for lunch afterwards. Mamá will not wish to lunch out, she never enjoys it, so if you send Roussos to fetch her when he leaves you, she can drive home in her own car and we can enjoy a celebration lunch.'

He had it all neatly cut and dried, Carey noted dryly, but she was more than willing to comply with what he had planned, and she nodded. Her cheeks were faintly flushed and her heart was already thudding hard and fast in anticipation of lunching with him. 'I'd like that,' she said unhesitatingly, and he smiled.

'I thought perhaps you might! This business will take some time, but we should be free by about one-thirty; can you keep yourself amused until then?'

'Quite easily!'

'One-thirty, then, at the Grande Brétagne.' He was still watching her in that curiously speculative way she had noticed a few minutes earlier. 'You seem a little—anxious,' he said quietly. 'Is there any reason why you should?'

She had been anxious, Carey recognised, but without any specific reason for it, and she shrugged, laughing it off because Niki was watching her too now. 'No reason at all,' she denied. 'I'm just naturally a bit on tenterhooks, that's all, hoping there won't be any last-minute snags.'

'There will not be,' Dimitri promised with a confidence she could not help but envy. He took Niki's hand and looked at his watch. 'My mother should be here by now; if you will go and see where she is, Carey, I——' He broke off when Madame Karamalis appeared, glancing again at his watch. 'Ah, Mamá, ine óra ná fíghoome!'

The old lady nodded. She was well aware that it was time they left, she prided herself on her punctuality, but she was obviously feeling rather emotional. Stooping to bring herself nearer to Niki's level, she stroked a light hand over his thick black curls, looking at him with sus-piciously bright eyes. She murmured something in Greek which Niki seemed to have difficulty understanding, al-though he nodded, and she looked at him with a tolerant smile.

'Ah, you do not always understand yet, eh, little one? Mikros ena—little one, yes?'

Obviously rather overwhelmed by the unaccustomed emotion, Niki looked up at Dimitri, clinging tightly to his hand meanwhile, and the fact that he turned to Dimitri and not to her, gave Carey a curious sense of loss suddenly.

It brought home to her the fact that some important part of her life was coming to an end and, no matter how delighted she was for Niki, for her own part she felt sad and vaguely tearful. Niki would never be quite so close to her again as he had been during those four years when she had been the most important person in his life, and she acknowledged that it *was* time for her to go.

'We will see you at one-thirty,' Dimitri was saying, and she hastily brought herself back to earth. A certain look in his eyes suggested that he realised something of what she was feeling, and just briefly he reached and took her hand, his long fingers enfolding hers and squeezing gently for a moment before he let go. '*Heréte*, Carey,' he said softly, and she smiled.

'*Heréte*,' she said, automatically responding in Greek, and wondered why his goodbye sounded so alarmingly final this time.

The chance of seeing someone she knew in the teeming streets of Athens was pretty remote in her case, Carey thought. Which was why she turned swiftly when she spotted a familiar face leaving the store she was about to enter, and followed Minerva back into the street. Pushing her way along the crowded pavement, trying to catch up, it wasn't until she was within touching distance that she stopped to consider what she was going to say.

It wasn't at all certain that Minerva would welcome her sudden appearance, but it had been irresistible to follow her, and as she came up alongside she placed a light hand on Minerva's arm. The moment she turned it was obvious that she was expecting someone else, and from the warm, soft look in her eyes it had to be the man who was by now probably her husband.

'Thespinis Gordon!' The eyes changed their expression to one of wariness, but years of inbred courtesy came to her aid and she proffered a hand. 'How do you do?'

'Very well, thank you, Kyria Petrakis.' Carey smiled,

taking a chance on using the name, a successful one judging by the faint flush that coloured Minerva's cheeks.

'You have learned my name,' she said, and Carey nodded.

'Dimitri told me.' There was an awkward pause, but Carey was not about to let the opportunity slip past her, and she was still smiling. 'I didn't expect to see you here in Athens, Kyria Petrakis, but I'm glad I did.'

'Dimitri had my letter?' Minerva asked, and already, Carey thought, she seemed just a little less wary, as if she remembered her sympathetic judgment of Aliki's situation and her own.

'Yes, he had it,' said Carey, then indicated a little café just beyond where they stood. 'Will you have coffee with me, Kyria Petrakis? I'm seeing Dimitri and Nikolas for lunch at one-thirty, but I've plenty of time before then. Will you join me?'

Minerva gave a deep sigh and shook her head, so that initially Carey thought she was refusing. Instead she was obviously condemning her own forgetfulness. 'But of course, it is today that Dimitri officially becomes Nikolas's father, is it not? I do not know how I could have forgotten such a thing.'

'We could drink to both happy occasions,' Carey suggested with a smile. 'Niki's future and your own happier one.'

'It *will* be happier,' Minerva insisted, and Carey was willing enough to believe her.

'I'm sure of it,' she said. 'So shall we drink to it, *kyria*?'

'I do not have much time,' Minerva told her with a quick glance at her wrist, 'but I will have coffee with you, Thespinís Gordon; *efharisto*.'

The café was fairly busy, but not overcrowded, and despite her initial check on the time, Minerva seemed in no special hurry once they were seated at one of the little tables. After two cups of coffee each and a couple of pastries thick with nuts and honey, she seemed much more relaxed; it was all the more unexpected, therefore, when it was Minerva who eventually raised the subject that both of them had been carefully avoiding ever since they came in.

'I hope that my letter to Dimitri made everything clear,' she said. 'I did not mention you by name, Thespinis Gordon, but it has troubled me a little since that Dimitri may have blamed you. That he may have realised who encouraged me and gave me the courage I needed. I do hope you were not involved, *thespinís*.'

While she licked honey from her fingers, Carey took a moment to decide just how frank she should be. It wasn't an easy subject to discuss, and yet it was what had been in the back of her mind when she caught up with Minerva. 'Actually he read part of your letter out to me,' she said. 'He *was* angry because he guessed I must have been the one who talked to you about Aliki; no one else would have the knowledge, he said, which of course was right. But he thought I'd deliberately influenced you knowing what you had in mind; fortunately I managed to convince him he was wrong.'

Minerva looked very contrite, shaking her head as she looked across at her. 'I am so sorry, *thespinís*, I would not have had that happen, I did not think.'

Anxious to reassure her, Carey smiled. 'Oh, please don't worry about it, Kyria Petrakis, it was soon cleared up.'

Minerva said nothing for a moment then she moistened her lips before she spoke, her eyes looking from below heavy lids. 'I know they will have been angry,' she said with unexpected confidence. 'Dimitri was, was he not?'

She really cared, Carey thought. Minerva was very fond of her autocratic family and she loved them despite their autocratic ways. Carey's thoughts at the moment were all on trying in some way to heal the breach between them, but she would need to tread very carefully, she realised. They all set such store by what Dimitri thought and said, and she could at least state that Dimitri had been not so much angry as hurt.

'He was hurt,' she said. 'He was much more hurt than angry, Kyria Petrakis, and I know that's so because he told me himself.' Minerva's eyes were downcast, her mouth slightly unsteady and Carey went on, choosing her words carefully. 'I wish you could have been there, and then you'd know what I mean. You see he—all of them, according to Dimitri, couldn't understand why you expected them to be angry when they were only anxious for you to be happy again with someone you love.'

'Mamá?' Minerva asked, and Carey looked at her curiously.

'I'm certain Madame Karamalis had been crying that morning when I saw her.'

Minerva's voice was soft, but she was shaking her head as if she found it hard to believe that her mother had wept for her. 'Mamá never wept for Aliki,' she said. 'How could I expect her to welcome my choice when she so firmly condemned Aliki's, and made us all follow her example?'

'Madame Karamalis?'

Carey was staring at her, scarcely able to believe it. She had, if she blamed anyone in the family for taking the decision for them all, blamed Dimitri as the strongest personality. That it had been Madame Karamalis who took the decision to cut Aliki off from her family had never even entered her head.

'You do not believe it?' A faint smile touched Minerva's mouth for a moment; a small, bitter smile that did not reach her eyes. 'Mamá is very—moral, Thespinís Gordon, and until the past few years she and not Dimitri made the decisions. Now he is very much the patriarch, and Mamá is as ready as any of us to listen to him.'

Carey was recalling that look of Dimitri's, the dark look of hurt in his eyes when he spoke of his sister, and she shook her head. 'I've never seen Dimitri look as he did that morning,' she said. 'I didn't realise how hurt he could be. He said you should have realised; you should have known them well enough to realise how happy they would have been to see you happily married again.'

Eyes downcast, Minerva shook her head. 'I believe it of Dimitri,' she said after a moment or two. 'He is a good man, Thespinís Gordon.' Then she glanced up suddenly and caught Carey unaware. 'But you know that, do you not? You are—close to him.'

Carey said nothing for the moment, but sat stirring her coffee round and round in the cup. How much did Minerva know and how much was she guessing at? she wondered, for Minerva might be as adept at reading the signs as her mother was. She started almost guiltily when a hand was laid over hers suddenly, and she looked up into Minerva's warm, appealing eyes.

'I do not intend to embarrass you, *thespinís*,' she said, 'please forgive me if I do. I know that Dimitri is attractive to women, and I have seen the way that you look sometimes when he is near——' Her long thin hands fluttered apologetically. 'I am sorry.'

'You don't embarrass me, Kyria Petrakis,' Carey hastened to assure her, and smiled faintly. 'I'm accustomed now to the Greek way of taking an interest in everyone's personal life, it's embarrassing at first, but rather endearing when one gets used to it.' She laughed lightly, reminding herself that she wouldn't be looking at Dimitri any way at all for very much longer. 'I shall feel quite alien when I go back to England in about a week's time.'

'You are going back?' Minerva looked surprised. 'I had thought Dimitri was firmly set on keeping you here. Nikolas will miss you,' she added, and took note of Carey's high colour.

'Not as much as I shall miss him,' Carey remarked ruefully. 'He's become very firmly attached to Dimitri, which is a good thing now that he's his son.'

'His son,' Minerva echoed faintly. 'Of all my brothers I love Dimitri best, for he is the most understanding and I believe he might have understood my feeling for Panos Petrakis.'

'A free and honest man,' Carey quoted, recalling Dimitri's assessment of his brother-in-law. 'That's how he described your husband, Kyria Petrakis. He said how much they would have enjoyed your wedding if only you hadn't run away.'

Quite clearly Minerva was holding her emotions under tight control and her eyes glistened darkly, so that Carey put forward her idea quickly, while she was still in the balance between regret and nostalgia. 'I should have known,' Minerva whispered.

'It isn't too late!' Carey leaned across the little table, almost willing her to understand and respond, 'I know that if you came home you'd be welcomed with open arms. It would be such a pity if this was allowed to drift and the gap widened, just for the want of someone making the first move. Please believe me, Kyria Petrakis, I know how often Aliki regretted not writing, trying to heal the breach, and her situation was much different from yours. Please—think about it, I beg you.'

Minerva's dark expressive eyes held hers for a moment, but she lacked the immediate courage to act impulsively as she had done when she eloped, and only now did Carey realise how deeply she had involved herself in something that had nothing at all to do with her. There was nothing she could do about it now, and perhaps when she was gone Dimitri might remember that she had been the one who restored his sister to them.

Picking up her cup, Minerva drank the last of her coffee, discreetly dabbed her lips then gathered up her handbag, and all without looking up. 'I will think about it,' she promised, and glanced at her wrist as she spoke. 'If you will please excuse me, Thespinís Gordon, I have to go.' She looked up at last and there was an unmistakable angle to her chin that made her look more truly Karamalis than Carey had ever seen her before. 'I am meeting my husband,' she said, and Carey found the pride with which she said it oddly touching.

Feeling as if it was something of an anti-climax after her impassioned appeal, Carey too got to her feet. Minerva had made no definite promise and she had hoped she would, so maybe nothing would come of her attempted peacemaking. But as she took Minerva's proffered hand she tried to judge what was going on behind those dark, heavy-lidded eyes.

That she had been affected, Carey had no doubt, but to what extent remained to be seen. The handclasp lingered and a small frown drew at fine black brows for a moment, then Minerva had that curiously anxious look again. 'If you——' She began, then shook her head and turned quickly to go. '*Heréte, thespinís!*'

Gazing after her, Carey flicked an anxious tongue over her lips, for she suddenly realised that her efforts might even be resented, and that it might be better if she said nothing about it. Very soon now she would have no further interest in the doings of the Karamalis family, and she just wished she felt more pleased about it.

Niki's exuberance during lunch took the form of an unending barrage of chatter that Carey hoped would do something to cover her own rather subdued mood. It wasn't that she was any less delighted with his happiness about being adopted, but ever since she had parted from Minerva she had been thinking about how little time she had left before she went away for good.

She had already decided that she wouldn't say anything to Dimitri about meeting Minerva, for it would serve no purpose except to give rise to disappointment if nothing happened. Minerva's manner had not been encouraging enough when she left her to indicate she would do as she suggested, and go and see her family.

Carey had eaten her way through a first course of fried whiting without really appreciating the crisp little fish as she usually did, Niki's voice chattering on meanwhile about what had happened and what was going to happen in the future. Papá had told him that he would soon be going to a different school, and that when he was bigger he should have a bicycle of his own.

He was happy, Carey told herself, as she started on a plateful of *pastitsio* without any real enthusiasm, and that was the most important thing. Dimitri would be good to him, she no longer doubted his motives, and the two of them would be happy together. No doubt in time there would be more than two of them, for she could not believe that Dimitri was destined to be single all his life, especially now that he had a child to care for. A wife would complete the family circle, but Carey didn't want to be around when that happened.

She started visibly when Dimitri laid a hand over hers and leaned towards her, and when she looked up his eyes had a questioning, speculative look that was very hard to meet. Having got her attention he shifted his gaze to the soft uncertainty of her mouth, and Carey felt a little shiver slip along her spine at the familiar magic of his touch.

'What is troubling you, Carey?'

His voice was so quiet that it made no impression at all on Niki's garrulous chatter, but Carey felt suddenly very exposed, as if he was trying to see into her mind, and she shook her head quickly. 'Nothing's troubling me,' she denied, though obviously without much conviction, for Dimitri's lips were pursed doubtfully.

'You lie, *mikros ena*,' he declared softly but without hesitation. 'Your eyes are evasive and your hands are trembling.' He pressed his strong fingers over hers in such a way that she felt bound to look up again. 'Is it because you will be leaving us in little more than a week from now? Are you regretting your determination to go, Carey?'

It was too close to her heart to answer easily, and she felt too vulnerable exposed to the gaze of a restaurant full of other people. Also Niki was likely to overhear, and he knew nothing of her plan yet. 'I—I'd rather not talk about it here and now,' she told him, glancing at Niki who was presently taking an interest in a very large woman at the next table while he consumed a mouthful of minced meat and macaroni.

'You have only yourself to blame if you have regrets,' Dimitri told her, and squeezed her fingers again when she looked like protesting. 'I have not sought to influence you this time, Carey, I am taking no part. It was your decision to give notice and only you can change it.'

In other words, Carey thought bitterly, he was going to make her ask him to keep her on if she had changed her mind, and she didn't dare do that, however desperately she wanted to. If she did he was shrewd enough to realise that it would not be entirely because of Niki. 'I—I shan't change my mind,' she insisted in a huskily small voice. 'You're a—a family now, you and Niki, and when you marry——'

'You think I shall marry?' Dimitri asked softly, but before she could reply Niki joined in, drawn by the mention of his name.

Darting his gaze from one to the other, he seemed to sense that something wasn't quite right, and he frowned. With a forkful of *pastitsio* poised ready to pop into his mouth, he looked at Carey. 'Aren't you hungry, Carey?' he asked, and she hastily summoned a half-smile.

'Not very,' she said. 'I had pastries with my coffee and it was very silly of me.'

'Are you coming to Piraeus with us?' he asked, completely at a loss to know why pastries should diminish one's appetite. 'Thíos—Papá is taking me to see the ships next week. We own some of them, did you know? We've got ships of our own!'

He was obviously impressed, but what touched Carey most was the fact that he still wanted to include her in their outings, and she found it very hard to answer him because her throat felt constricted. Also Dimitri was watching her as intently as Niki was, she realised, and with two pairs of dark eyes waiting for her to say whether or not she was going with them to see the ships, she simply couldn't find the words.

'Don't you want to see our ships?' Niki demanded, and she shook her head slowly as she struggled with a lump in her throat.

'I—I can't, Niki,' she managed, after what seemed an interminable time. 'I—I have a lot to do during the next week.'

'What have you got to do?'

Oh, those familiar, endless questions! Carey thought wildly as she struggled for composure. 'I have to get ready, Niki.' She saw the questions looming and Dimitri was no longer taking any part in the conversation, he wasn't going to help her.

'You going somewhere?' Niki asked suspiciously, and she nodded.

She no longer made any pretence of eating, but sat with her hands clenched tightly either side of her plate, and her eyes bright with tears she was determined not to shed in a place as public as a restaurant full of people. She longed for Dimitri to come to her rescue, for she couldn't bring herself to tell Niki the truth, not in the present circumstances, and she closed her eyes in a brief, wordless prayer of thanks when he did just that.

'Carey has decided to go back to England, Nikolas,' he told him, very quietly and quite without emotion, she noticed, and kept her eyes downcast when in the silence that followed she felt Niki's reproachful eyes on her.

'Why?' he asked, inevitably, and this time Dimitri left her to answer for herself.

'It had to happen one day,' she explained in a small shaky voice that betrayed tears as surely as the misty brightness of her eyes did. 'I was never—I didn't intend staying as long as I have, and now that you have a *papá* you don't need a nanny.'

Niki's bottom lip was quivering, but he bit on it determinedly, and only his huge reproachful eyes showed how he felt. 'When I had a *mamá* you stayed,' he reminded her, and he was quite plainly indignant that she thought him simple enough to accept such a blatantly thin excuse. 'You lived with us when I had a *mamá*, so I don't see why not when I have a *papá*?'

He was as emotional as all the Karamalises were, and his tears were less likely to be held back as determinedly as hers were. But this was not something she had anticipated having to cope with in a public place. At home she could have cuddled him to her and tried to make him see, but she felt helpless in the present situation and didn't know what to say to him. Her predicament was made worse because Dimitri was doing absolutely nothing to help, and in those few minutes while she struggled to find words, Carey almost hated him.

'That was different, Niki.' She chose each word carefully, because she couldn't be exactly sure what effect they would have. 'You see, darling, Mamá was differently placed. One day your *papá* will marry and then you'll have a *mamá* again as well, and you won't need a nanny at all, do you see now?'

'Who?' Niki demanded, and with his lips pursed he looked quite uncannily like the man beside him. 'Why does Papá have to get married when we've got you?'

She couldn't go on', Carey realised. Not with Dimitri sitting there and doing nothing to help her while she was being torn apart, as if it didn't matter at all to him that she couldn't cope. Even if the situation was more or less of her own making, he could have shown some compassion, and his not doing so was her undoing.

She got up from the table hastily, without giving Dimitri time to get to his feet as he would normally have done, and murmured an excuse, then went blindly off in the direction of the powder-room, avoiding the intervening tables only by a miracle.

'Carey.'

His voice followed her. Discreetly quiet but loud enough to reach her, and she knew he couldn't follow because it would mean leaving Niki alone at the table. She wasn't even sure that he would have followed anyway, she thought bitterly, and wondered how she could love a man who stood by and let her struggle with the result of something he had begun. Yet not for a moment did she deny that she loved him, not any longer, and that was the hardest thing of all to bear as she sat miserably in front of a mirror and gazed at her own unhappy face.

Carey was feeling rather guilty for having dimmed the excitement and happiness of Niki's big day, but the fact of living in Greece seemed to have made her almost as emotionally volatile as the Greeks themselves. None of them had said very much on the drive back from Athens and several times she had been on the verge of telling them both how sorry she was to have dampened the celebration. Then at the last minute she had lacked the nerve to do even that.

She sat beside Dimitri in the front seat as usual, and tried to keep as far away from him as it was possible to get in the front of a car, but every turn in the winding country road brought a moment of contact that set her pulses racing and her heart thudding like a drum in her breast. How could he fail to realise how she felt about him when every look and gesture felt like a betrayal of her love for him?

He had looked anxious when she rejoined them in the restaurant, and she had found it hard to believe, for anxiety was not an emotion she would have attributed to Dimitri. And when he had helped her into the car his hand had held hers for longer than was strictly necessary, while his black eyes tried to make her look at him. Something she had avoided doing for fear he saw something in her eyes that would give her away.

There could be no question of her changing her mind about going, for she could no longer bear to be in such close proximity to a man who could turn from a moment of passion, as she had seen Dimitri do, and the next moment appear cool and perfectly in control. It was no longer parting from Niki that was the cause of her heart-ache, but leaving Dimitri; yet the sooner she was away from him the better.

They were driving along the narrow shrub-lined access road to the villa when Niki leaned over the back of her seat and touched a small hand to her cheek. 'You all better, Carey?' he asked, and she nodded, managing a brief smile as well.

'Yes, thank you, darling. We're home now and you'll be able to tell Yayá Karamalis all about that big lunch you had, won't you?'

He was looking at her and his dark eyes were troubled. If only she could have handled things better back there in the restaurant it need not have been quite so traumatic for either of them. Niki was going to miss her, no matter how attached to Dimitri he had become, and she was far more of an emotional coward than she had realised. He still had a hand resting on her shoulder when the car glided smoothly to a halt in front of the house.

'What you going to do now?' he asked, while he waited for Dimitri to let him out of the back of the car, and Carey shook her head.

Dimitri, however, spoke up unhesitatingly. 'I shall be talking to Carey in the small *salon* for a while,' he told Niki, 'so do not come in and interrupt if you please. Do as Carey says and tell Yaya about lunch; I am certain she will be interested to hear just how much one small boy can consume in a little over an hour!'

Carey did not look up, even when strong fingers squeezed her arm as she was helped from the car, and she knew it was no good telling him that she was in no mood for any more exchanges. Instead she took Niki's hand as they went up the front steps and smiled at him rather absently. 'Do as Papá says,' she told him as they walked into the hall. 'I'll see you later.'

But he clung to her hand still, suspicious and anxious, his dark eyes wide and appealing. 'You won't go without telling me, Carey?' he pleaded, and Carey swallowed hard before she could answer him.

'No, of course I won't, darling. I'm not going just yet, not until next week, but I have a lot to do first. Getting tickets for the flight and packing, you know all the things we had to do——' She stopped short, a lump in her throat when she recalled their coming to Greece. 'Run along and find Yayá, Niki, and don't forget to speak distinctly when you have to use English.'

He nodded, distracted now by the thought of telling his grandmother all about the new school he was to go to, and the bicycle he was going to have one day. As she turned from watching him Carey sighed inwardly, for she wondered if after all he would miss her for very long once she was gone. And she sighed again, for quite a different reason, when she looked across and noticed that the door of the small *salon* had been left open for her.

Dimitri was sitting on the small table he used as a desk on occasions, and lighting a cheroot, and he looked up when she came in, narrowing his eyes against the curling blue smoke. 'Are you going to refuse to sit down?' he asked as she came half-way across the room and then stood watching him uneasily.

'Not if you don't mind me sitting in one of the armchairs by the window.' He extended a hand in invitation and she walked over and perched herself on the very edge of the leather seat, facing the window and looking out at the garden at the front of the house. 'I don't know what you have to say to me,' she said in a small, hesitant voice, 'but I'd rather not talk any more about leaving if you don't mind.'

He remained where he was, sitting on the edge of the table and looking across at her through the drift of smoke from his cheroot, and in contrast to her obvious uncertainty he spoke quietly but with confidence. 'I regret that more than I can say—no, please, do not disagree with me, Carey. I had no intention that you should become so upset, I had not realised how—deeply you felt about leaving Nikolas or I would not have mentioned it. Please believe that.'

'I believe it.'

His apology was something else that disturbed her, for she had never seen him as a man who apologised easily and he was obviously genuinely sorry that she had been so upset during lunch. 'You are feeling better now? This conversation can be delayed until you feel more able to cope with it, if you prefer.'

Carey shook her head dazedly. This wasn't all the kind of confrontation she had anticipated, and she wasn't sure she *could* cope, but she wouldn't back down now and make him think she was some kind of weak-willed, weepy female who collapsed in tears at the slightest provocation. 'I'm perfectly all right, thank you.'

He was silent for a moment or two, taking long draws at the cheroot and expelling clouds of smoke that began to tickle her nose even across the other side of the room. Then he tapped off a long nub of ash and spoke as he did it, without looking at her. 'You are not aware that Andoni has been given the London office, of course,' he said, and Carey made a hasty decision whether or not to admit to already knowing.

Instead she compromised. 'That will please Rhoda,' she guessed. 'She can have her town house after all.' Hands clasped tightly on her lap, Carey wondered how far she dared go. She was on the verge of leaving so she could take a chance, and it wouldn't really matter if she offended anyone. 'Mitso told me that you wouldn't give Andoni the London office because for one thing he was too useful here, and for another because he doesn't speak English well enough,' she said. 'I don't understand what made you change your mind—not that it's any of my business, of course,' she added hastily, and realised that Dimitri was dismissing the adjoinder with a wave of his hand.

'I wished to have Rhoda away from here,' he told her in a quiet voice that somehow sent little trickles of ice sliding along her spine as she listened to it, and she dared not look at him. 'I do not like such viciousness as she displayed when she slapped you, and it was better to let Andoni have the London office and Rhoda her town house than have the two of you under one roof.'

Carey's heart was beating so hard and fast she found it difficult to breathe, and her face was flushed with warm colour that she could do nothing to hide, even though she gazed down at the hands on her lap. 'I—I won't be here for much longer,' she reminded him in a husky whisper, and she had never regretted anything as much as her hasty decision to leave.

Dimitri took another long draw at the cheroot and expelled smoke from between pursed lips, while heavy-lidded eyes fixed themselves on her immovably. 'I had not thought you so serious about leaving,' he told her, and again the softness of his voice touched her like a physical caress.

'Would it have made a difference?' she whispered, looking up at last, and Dimitri was gouging out the cheroot with a ruthlessness that sent a shiver along her spine. It was instinctive to get to her feet when he straightened up and stood looking at her for a moment before starting across the room. She was trembling like a leaf and her hands clasped and unclasped anxiously as she stood with her eyes downcast. 'Dimitri, if I can——'

She broke off quickly when a sudden babble of Greek voices out in the hall all but drowned what she was saying, and like Dimitri she stared across at the door. She was only a second or two behind him in recognising one particular voice in the crescendo of sound, and the tears that had been so long under control brimmed into her eyes from sheer pleasure.

'Minerva!' she breathed. 'She came!' Dimitri was stunned, staring at the closed door as if he was rooted to the spot, and she placed a hand over his arm, gently urging him across. 'Go and welcome her,' she whispered, not for a moment seeing the incongruity of her telling Dimitri what he should do. 'Let her see how glad you are she came—it's *you* she'll depend on to see her through this.'

The excitement in the hall was growing, and someone laughed; a hard, brittle laugh that Carey thought she recognised as Rhoda's, then her hand slid from Dimitri's arm as he turned and went striding over to the door. She stood watching him, her heart hammering wildly, knowing that if she had to go in a week's time she had at least done this for him, and as the tears shimmered on her lashes Dimitri turned and looked back at her.

'Wait here!' he instructed before he turned to open the door, and there was nothing Carey could do about the laughter that welled up and burst from her as it closed behind him.

CHAPTER NINE

In fact Carey didn't stay where she was, because she thought it very unlikely that Dimitri would be coming back very soon, and the prospect of just sitting about in one small room didn't appeal at all. When she crossed the hall on her way upstairs she could hear voices in the *salon*; not quite so loud now, but still talking several at a time and edged with that suggestion of excitable aggression that typified Greek conversation. She couldn't hear Niki, but he would be there, probably slightly overwhelmed by all

the excitement and sticking close to Dimitri or his grandmother.

As far as Carey was concerned Minerva's arrival had
given rise to a curious sense of intangibility, of waiting for
something to happen, and it made her so restless that she
didn't know what to do with herself. In her bedroom she
stood for a moment taking stock of her reflected image in
the mirror, and wondering if she really was fool enough to
ask Dimitri to let her stay on. She was sure he would, but
the question was whether anything had really changed
enough to make it worthwhile.

It was true he claimed to have changed his mind about
giving Andoni the London office because he objected to
the way Rhoda had behaved towards her, but Carey felt
it would be taking a lot for granted if she read too much
into it. Dimitri was autocratic and he was not over-fond of
his sister-in-law, so that she told herself he was just as
likely to have made the arrangement for his own benefit
as for hers.

Still undecided and more restless than ever, she sighed
as she turned from the mirror and consulted her wristwatch. The family reunion was unlikely to break up much
before it was time for the evening meal, and that was not
for several hours yet, so she had better find something to
keep herself occupied until then.

From her window she caught a glimpse of a distant
hillside, and of light, honey-coloured pillars set among the
trees, and for a moment she was tempted. No one would
mind if she borrowed one of the cars and a chauffeur for
an hour, and went to visit the little temple of Artemis, but
nostalgia of that kind, she decided as she closed her bedroom door behind her, was pointless. She would be much
better occupied sitting by the pool with a book.

A little over an hour later a lot of pages had been turned,
but Carey had no idea what the book was about because
she simply couldn't concentrate on it. Yet she was instantly
alert when she heard footsteps on the path through the

shrubbery, coming her way. Firm and easily recognisable footsteps that brought a sudden lurching beat to her heart, and made her hands tremble so much that the pages of the book rustled like leaves.

Because she knew who it was, she didn't look up, not even when a long dark shadow fell across her, but she gasped aloud when he reached down and took the book from her hands. 'Dimitri!'

She said it in such a shaky voice that it must have given away exactly how she was feeling, and as Dimitri seated himself on the chair next to hers he was smiling faintly. Closing the book carefully, he laid it on the seat beside him. 'Do not pretend you are surprised,' he told her, and leaned forward with his elbows resting on his knees, his black, heavy-lidded eyes watching her steadily. 'I expected to find you in the small *salon*,' he went on, and Carey almost laughed aloud at the idea of him actually expecting her to wait exactly where he had told her to.

'For how long?' Just for a moment she met his eyes and her pulse stirred in such violent response that she caught her breath. 'Family reunions have a habit of going on a bit, so I thought I'd better amuse myself.'

He picked up the book and eyed its somewhat garish cover for a moment, then arched a brow at her. 'With a book about murder?' he asked, and she laughed in spite of herself.

'I almost borrowed a car and went out, but then I decided I wouldn't.'

'Do you want to go out again?'

He asked the question in the voice that could play havoc with her emotions and Carey hung on tightly to her common sense, sitting a little more upright in her chair because it made her feel more in control. 'It was seeing it from my bedroom window,' she told him. 'I thought I might go and see the little temple again before I leave.'

'Ah! The temple of Artemis at Naós Lófos?'

She nodded, aware of the black eyes watching her

closely and of the hard pounding beat of her own heart.
'No particular reason,' she assured him hastily. 'I just saw
it and remembered how pretty it was.'

'And how affecting?' Dimitri suggested quietly, and her
reply was made with a certain naïve frankness.

'That's why I didn't go.'

He said nothing, but got up from his chair after a
moment or two, and Carey stared at the big hands that
were thrust in front of her and curved invitingly. 'Come,'
he said with that familiar hint of impatience. 'If you want
to go and see the temple of Artemis again I will take you.
It will be my way of saying thank you for persuading
Minerva to come and see us.' She took his hands and he
drew her up from her chair, holding her as she stood close
against him, with their clasped hands at their sides. 'You
must have cared,' he said softly, 'to have achieved this,
and we are all very grateful to you, Carey.'

He bent his head and lightly touched his lips to hers,
then looked deep into her eyes while Carey tried hard to
keep control of her reeling senses. As always Dimitri could
put everything out of her mind but his own nearness, and
the longing she felt was like a physical ache that weakened
her limbs and banished any thought she had had of leaving
him.

'Come,' he said, turning and drawing her along with
him. 'We will go and pray at the altar of Artemis, eh?'

'A pagan goddess?' Carey questioned lightly, and
Dimitri looked down at her with steady black eyes.

'*Our* goddess,' he murmured.

They drove in silence and in the kind of fat golden
afternoon that had been her first impression of the Villa
Karamalis. The Midas touch of the sun gilding the little
white houses along the road, and glazing the azure sky
with a copper sheen until it looked not quite real, and to
Carey's dazed way of thinking, the Olympus of the gods
must have been born of a moment like this.

The wind on the wooded hillside was cooler and the

sun less intense than the last time they climbed together, but as then Dimitri's hand helped her up the steepest parts towards the summit. Pausing as she had on the first occasion to look at the overall impression before they went inside, Carey felt she had never seen a more beautiful place, nor would she ever, because nowhere else had the same meaning to her.

'It's beautiful,' she breathed, and lifted her face to the cooling wind off the distant sea. 'I shall never get tired of looking at it!'

'Never?'

Dimitri's question reminded her that as things stood at the moment she would have very little time to grow tired of it, for in a few days she would be gone. Away from Greece and out of Dimitri's life for good; it was something she didn't want to be reminded of, and she shook her head as she freed her hand and walked on alone into the temple.

It was all just as before, as it had been for most of time, but with the shadows deeper and more dramatic, and that impression of being on the edge of eternity more affecting than before. She paused briefly before the altar with its broken goddess lurking in the shadows, and a shiver slipped along her spine.

In the broken archway she stood and looked down at the steep hillside and the ancient steps, wide and worn with the feet of women desperate for sons to please their husbands, and she turned swiftly and instinctively at the touch of a warm body against her back. Her heart beat so hard she could scarcely breathe, and her lips were parted as she looked over her shoulder into Dimitri's deep black eyes.

'Do you still feel the magic?' he asked, and the softness of his voice lightly skimmed along her back like a caressing finger as she nodded understanding.

'Don't you?' she whispered, and turned again to look down the steep hillside.

'Iphigenia,' Dimitri murmured, and his sudden husky laughter jolted her heart into wild confusion. 'Not the virginal Artemis, I think,' he said. 'Not here, with us, eh, my lovely?'

His hand touched lightly on her neck and she shivered. Lifting her hair, he wound it into a knot as he had done on that first occasion, but instead of resting it on her neck he pulled it apart and ran his fingers through its silky thickness until it was a wild tangled mass about her face and neck.

'You would not be a virginal goddess, would you, Carey?'

With him, Carey thought, she had no desire at all to be a virginal goddess or a goddess of any kind; she longed to be a woman, the kind of woman Dimitri wanted. 'I'm not a goddess,' she denied, her voice small and not quite steady, 'I'm a woman; just an ordinary woman, except that here—here I feel something special because of the magic of this place.'

'And because you *are* perhaps something special,' Dimitri suggested.

If only she was, Carey thought longingly, perhaps she need not be brought so sharply back to earth this time. Every breath she took seemed to bring closer contact with him, and the hard, rhythmic beat of his heart felt like part of her own body, making it difficult to distinguish between the two.

'*Agape mou!*'

My love. The endearment was whispered against her ear and Carey half closed her eyes when the warmth of his breath caressed her skin. Her whole body was pliant and yielding, longing for the arms that at last slid around her and drew her to him, long fingers gentle on the soft curves that swelled towards them. He burned her like fire, and she surrendered to the fire with a fervour of desire she could neither resist nor deny.

His mouth touched lightly on her neck and she made a

little moan of pleasure, complying eagerly when he turned her within the circle of his arms. For a moment he looked down into her face, bright and flushed and almost naïvely anxious as his mouth hovered above her lips with a promise she longed to have fulfilled.

He pressed her closer still, and the fierce virility of him demanded a surrender she was only too willing to make as she arched her body in soft, yielding compliance to the strength of his arms. Lifting her arms, she wound them around his neck. "Dimitri!"

She had only time enough to whisper his name once before he lowered his head, taking her mouth with the passionate fierceness she had longed for, possessing it so completely that she seemed to have stopped breathing, and lay still and unresisting in his arms. Light, gentle, eager hands eased open her dress and he laid warm palms on her neck, looking at her with glowing dark eyes as he slipped them down to her shoulders and bared her pale skin to the richness of the sun.

'Carey. Carey, *mikros ena mou*—my little one.' He pressed his lips to the pulse at the side of her neck and his mouth lingered, touching lightly on the softness of her shoulders and the warm swell of her breasts, until her head was spinning. 'Carey, will you leave me? Will you leave me the unhappiest man in Greece? *Can* you leave me, *agape mou?*'

Her eyes swimmingly soft and heavy-lidded, Carey looked up at him, her fingers curling into the thickness of black hair above his ears. '*Will* you be unhappy?' she whispered, and met those black eyes with a steadiness that would have surprised her at any other time but this.

'You know it!'

But she was shaking her head, too anxious to have it clear just how he felt to take anything for granted. 'I don't know anything except—except how *I* feel,' she said, and Dimitri took her face between his hands and looked down into her eyes.

There was passion there, but something else too. A warm, tender look that she had never seen before and which aroused such responses in her she wanted to reach up and draw that dark head down to her breast. She loved him and she no longer made any attempt to hide it from him; if he did not feel as she did then it was all over and she would go back to England, even though she left a part of herself there with him.

One arm encircled her waist again and the other hand reached up to wind strands of tangled, silky fair hair around his fingers. 'I did not know how you felt until Minerva came home,' he told her in that deep, quietly affecting voice. 'When I heard her out there in the hall, and you so obviously knew something about her being there, I knew—I *hoped* that you had gone to so much effort because you knew how I felt. You knew how much it hurt me that she had run away, and I remembered the look in your eyes that morning.' He pressed a strand of hair to his lips and looked deep into her eyes. 'Am I wrong, my love?'

How could she deny it? Carey shook her head, her grey eyes soft and shining and she smiled. 'You looked so hurt,' she whispered. 'I didn't realise you were so—vulnerable, and I already loved you; what else could I do except try and persuade Minerva to come home?'

'Carey.' He said it softly and the cadence he gave her name was like music. 'Carey, I have loved you for so long now it seems I must have begun to love you the moment you walked into my life. I think Nikolas will be pleased that we are to be married, for now he will know you will *not* be leaving him, ever.'

'You're going to marry me?' Her eyes laughed at him, teasing him for his arrogant assumption that she would marry him.

'You think me too proud?' Dimitri demanded, and the hand in her hair grasped tightly suddenly so that she objected, laughing as she tried to free herself. 'Did I not tell you, *kopéla*, that the Karamalis have a different kind of pride?'

She was drawn into his arms again and held with a fiercely possessive force that threatened to crush her ribs, and his mouth when it took hers had the same bruising hardness in the first few moments. Then she put her arms up around his neck and stroked her fingers where the black hair grew thickest at the back of his head, and his kiss gentled to a less brutal force.

With his mouth against her neck he whispered softly in his own tongue and when he at last lifted his head again, his eyes looked down at her with a glowing darkness that lifted her heart. 'Stay with me, my little love,' he murmured. 'Marry me and I promise that you will never regret not going home.'

Gently, lovingly, Carey pulled his head down to her and whispered with her lips against his. 'Home is where the heart is,' she reminded him. 'So I must stay here where you are, my love.'

'Oh, blessed Artemis,' Dimitri murmured, as if the ancient goddess had indeed answered his prayer, and drew her into his arms again.

Harlequin Plus
A WORD ABOUT THE AUTHOR

When British-born and -bred Rebecca Stratton left school, she began a series of jobs that included everything—from punch-card operator to machinist in a suspender factory! But for her, there was only one real goal: someday she was going to be a professional writer.

And at long last, when she was forty-five, she left a safe and secure job to devote all her time to writing. Her first book, a romantic novel, was sent off to a publisher, and while waiting for a reply she completed two more manuscripts. Then came the joyous news: her first novel, *The Golden Madonna* (Romance #1748) had been accepted. She was on her way!

For Rebecca Stratton, a writing career means interviews by the local papers and speaking engagements before local clubs. But most of all, and best of all, it means settling down to the real nitty gritty: plain hard work.